# Idol

# Gossip

Book Three
in the
H3RO Series

An Atlantis Entertainment Novel

## J. S. Lee

Axellia Publishing

First Edition, December 2018
Published by Axellia Publishing

Print ISBN: 978-1-912644-17-9
eBook ASIN: B07K5VPN4C

Cover design by Natasha Snow Designs;
www.natashasnowdesigns.com

Edited by C. Lesley
Proofread by S. Harvell

This book is a work of fiction. Any references to historical events,
real people, or real locations are used fictitiously. Other
characters, names, places and incidents are the product of the
author's imagination. Any resemblances to actual events,
locations, or persons—living or dead—is entirely coincidental.

# CONTENTS

# DEDICATION

This book is dedicated to the following idols whose visuals helped inspire H3RO and bring this series to life, and added to the soundtrack which allowed me to write:

Bang Yongguk
Song Kyungil
Kang Insoo
Kim Sehyoon (Wow)
Son Dongwoon

And the dangerous maknae
Im Changkyun (IM)

# THE ATLANTIS ENTERTAINMENT UNIVERSE

Reverse Harem
(As J. S. Lee)

## *H3RO*

Idol Thoughts
Idol Worship
Idol Gossip

## *Onyx*

ONYX: Truth
ONYX: Heart
ONYX: Love
ONYX: Unity
ONYX: Forever

Young Adult Contemporary Romance
(As Ji Soo Lee)

## *Zodiac*

The Idol Who Became Her World
The Girl Who Gave Him The Moon
The Dancer Who Saved Her Soul
The Leader Who Fell From The Sky

*Coming Soon*

The Boy Who Showed Her The Stars

**Serenity Ackles & J. S. Lee**
Urban Fantasy Reverse Harem

***The Goddess of Fate & Destiny***

Cursed Luck
Stolen Luck

*Coming Soon*

Twisted Luck
Chosen Luck

# K-101

For those of you unfamiliar with K-Pop / K-Dramas / Korean culture, here's a short handy guide:

## Names

Names in Korean are written family name then given name. It's not uncommon to use the full name when addressing a person—even one you're close to.

박현태 is the Korean way of writing Park Hyuntae (Tae). Tae is pronounced like Tay.

권민혁 is the Korean way of writing Kwon Minhyuk

하균구 is the Korean way of writing Ha Kyungu (Kyun)

송준기 is the Korean way of writing Song Junki (Jun)

Nate and Dante are a little different as they are American-Korean and Chinese. Nate isn't a Korean name and would therefore be spelled out phonetically in Korean. The same for Dante. (For those curious, it would be 네이트 for Nate, and 단테 for Dante.)

## Surnames (Family names)

As the western worlds combined, we ended up with a lot of variation in surnames. In Korea, although there is variation, you will find a lot Kims, Lees, and Parks. To try to keep things as easy to follow as possible, I have tried to make sure that all characters don't have the same surname *unless* they're in the same family—like Holly. However, in reality, this is most often not the case.

BTS, for example have Kim Namjoon (RM), Kim Seokjin (Jin), and Kim Taehyung (V). They all share the same family name, but are not related.

## Oppa (오빠), hyung (형), noona (누나), and oennie (언니)

This one gets a little confusing at first. The first thing you need to know, in Korea, age is a very important thing. It's not uncommon for you to be asked your age before your name because you need to be spoken to with the correct level of respect (known as honorifics). To show this, there's actually several ways to speak to address a person and it usually depends on your age (an exception to this might be in a place of work where someone younger than you is more senior to you). But I'll keep this simple and limit myself to terms used in the book.

Traditionally, oppa, hyung, noona, and unnie are terms used to describe your older sibling—depending on what sex you are and what sex they are. If you are male, your older brother is hyung and your older sister is noona. If you are female, your older brother is your oppa, and your older sister is unnie (technically, 언니 when Romanized is oenni, but unnie has become a more standard way of writing this). However, this can often be transferred to people you are close to. A girl will call her older boyfriend oppa. An idol will call his older groupmates hyung.

## Sunbae (선배) and Hoobae (후배)

Along the same vein, sunbae (senior) and hoobae (junior)

may be used as an alternative when using experience as a basis, rather than age.

**Other**

**Comeback**: this is an odd one for most people. Your next single isn't just your next single. It's a comeback—and it doesn't matter if you've waited two months or two years.

**Kakao**: Kakao is a messaging app similar to Whatsapp or Wechat.

**SNS**: What we would call Social Media, Koreans use the term Social Networking Service. Included in this would be **V Live**, an app which allows Korean idols to communicate with their fans (a bit like Instagram Live)

**화이팅**: Fighting, or 'hwaiting' is a word commonly used as encouragement, like 'good luck' or 'let's do this'.

**Maknae**: a term used for the youngest member of a group.

**'Ya!'**: The Korean equivalent to 'Hey!'

**제 X 장**: Chapter (pronounced jae X jang)

Character Bios are also available at the back of this book

More terms and information is available on Ji Soo's website:
www.jislooleeauthor.com/k101

# 제1 장

# H3R오

*Baby I'm Sorry*

Tae opened the door and stepped in. Before Nate could follow, Kyun had pushed Tae to the side and swung his fist at Nate, hitting him in the eye. Then things descended into chaos.

All rational thought just left me and I stood there, screaming at everyone to stop like a deranged banshee.

Dante jumped in, getting his arms under Kyun's shoulders and dragging him away from Nate before Kyun could hit him again. Tae was right behind him, yelling at them both to calm down. Minhyuk went to Nate to make sure he was OK.

And then Jun was with me, pulling me outside, out of the way. "Stay here," he instructed me.

I shook my head. I knew why they were fighting, and if this was all my fault, I needed to try to fix it. I ducked past Jun and into the dorm. He followed me in, shutting the door behind us.

"Has it ever occurred to you that I should be the one punching you?" Nate snapped at Kyun, rubbing at his jaw.

"Holly got hurt because you couldn't keep it in

your pants!" Kyun yelled at him. Dante had let go of him, but he was very clearly standing with him to make sure he didn't go for Nate again.

"What in God's name is going on here?" Tae demanded. Judging from the expressions on everyone's faces, he was the only one who didn't have a clue.

Kyun leaned down, grabbing an iPad which had been discarded on the couch beside them and practically shoved it in Tae's face. Tae took it from him, scrolling through something.

"What is that?" I asked, now the confused one.

"It's all over the SNS and media," Minhyuk sighed, almost apologetically as Tae walked over to give me the iPad. I didn't miss the look he gave Nate as he passed him.

I took the device and felt my blood run cold. The first thing I saw was the image of me being punched by Nate. I started scrolling. The next picture was of Nate and the mystery woman all over each other in the club. That one hurt more than being punched in the face.

Nate turned, looking over my shoulder at the screen. "Who is she?"

"Who is she?" Kyun exploded. "You punched Holly!"

"It was an accident," I told him, calmly. "A guy grabbed me and Nate came to help. Unfortunately, because he was drugged, he hit me." I was surprised at how I sounded. It was almost like I was listening to someone else speak.

"Is that who drugged me?" Nate asked.

"She looks familiar," Jun added, peering over. I looked at him, and his eyes went wide with recognition. "Yes! She isn't the girl who was throwing eggs at you, but she's been at all our appearances."

"Are you sure?" I asked, staring at the woman. I never paid much attention to the crowds, but it seemed odd that she would turn up at the club where we were.

"I would say Nate has a sasaeng."

I gave Tae a wary looked. "A *sasaeng*? Really?" A sasaeng was an extreme fan—the crazy ones that obsessed over an idol and pretty much stalked them. Although they were technically the opposite of an anti-fan, supposedly doing whatever they did because they loved their favorite idol so much, I personally classed them as the same thing. I certainly didn't like the idea of tagging the word 'fan' on there.

"She claims she's dating Nate, and has been for some time," Tae shrugged.

Could things possibly get any worse?

No sooner did that thought cross my mind, I regretted it. They did.

"I'm not dating her, I'm dating Holly," Nate said, pulling a face. "The whole article is bullshit."

The room fell deathly silent and slowly, all eyes fell on Nate.

"Oh, this isn't good," I heard Jun mutter.

"You can't be dating her," Tae frowned. "She's with me."

"OK, how about we focus on this article and Nate's sasaeng?" Jun asked, brightly. Five faces ignored him, all turning to face me.

The knot in my stomach seemed to have been replaced with something equally as big, but spikey. "Holly, what's going on?" Kyun asked me, his expression dark.

I swallowed. Or I tried. There seemed to be some

form of cactus in there. "I …" I tried.

"I don't think this is the important thing here," Jun said again. I wanted to hug him, but at the same time, I wanted to warn him to keep away. I also wanted to know why he was so eager to change the subject.

"It's not," Dante told him. "Or it wouldn't be for you if she wasn't with you either." There was something in Jun's expression which had Dante's eyebrows shooting into his hairline. "She is?"

"I can explain," I said, weakly. That was a lie—I had no idea where to start with any of this.

"Please do," said Tae, coldly.

This was it. This was the moment I had been dreading. "First of all, please don't turn on each other," I begged. "The one in the wrong was me. None of you knew what was happening with each other, so if you're going to hate someone, that should be me. I deserve it." I could feel the tears building in the corner of my eyes, and I did my best to blink them away: I deserved this. "I didn't set out to hurt anyone, and then I started to get my senses together, I realized I was falling in love with you all. I really didn't want to hurt anyone, but I didn't know how I could choose."

"Who says you have to?" Jun asked, quietly.

"What?" Dante asked. "Have to what?"

"Choose," Jun shrugged.

"At this point, I think the decision is made for me," I told him. "And I understand that."

Jun shook his head. "No, I mean, why should you have to choose?" he said again.

This time it was Nate's turn to sigh. "Jun, we've been over this. I don't see how this could work."

"How what could work?" Kyun demanded. "And

what do you mean you've been over it. Did you two know?"

Despite everything that was happening, I couldn't stop my eyes going between Jun and Nate. I'd had a suspicion for a long time that Jun knew, even though he had continued to spend time with me. He'd kissed me—and more than that. But Nate too?

"I told Jun I had feelings for Holly," Nate admitted. "A while later he admitted the same, and that he thought you guys did too. I didn't believe it, especially not after I slept with Holly."

"*You* slept with Holly?" Kyun cried in disbelief.

Minhyuk held his hands up as Dante put a warning hand on Kyun's arm. "I want to hear this out."

"You too?" Kyun asked. When Minhyuk nodded, Kyun shook his arm free of Dante's grip and stalked over to the television, glowering at everyone from the far side of the room.

"What is there to hear out?" Tae asked. "Holly can't be with all of us. She needs to pick one."

My mouth fell open. Pick one? Tae still wanted something between us after all this? Even more astonishing was he thought I would be able to choose. That was part of what had put me in this mess to start with.

"Who says she has to, hyung?" Jun asked, carefully.

"Me, for one," Kyun snorted.

"Let's hear Jun out," Minhyuk insisted.

"There is no need to listen to any more nonsense from the maknae," Kyun said, shooting a look at the member in question.

"No, I want to hear this too," Dante said, quietly.

"It's not difficult," Jun shrugged. "We all like Holly. She likes all of us. Why make her choose? Why can't she be with all of us?"

"There is no amount of money on this earth that will ever have you and I hooking up," Kyun said, firmly.

Jun pulled a face. "That's not what I mean."

"She's with all of us, but not at the same time," Nate sighed, turning to Jun. "See, I told you that they would never go for it."

"Are you saying you'd be happy with that?" Minhyuk asked Nate, tilting his head.

"I wasn't sure," Nate told him. "Last night, I almost decided on a flat-out no when Holly said she had been with Kyun."

"And now?"

He looked at me, then back to Minhyuk, slowly nodding. "I'd at least want to try."

"I'd be able to do it," Jun declared, folding his arms. "I've known the whole time."

"You're an idiot," Kyun said, rolling his eyes.

"I would need to think about it," Minhyuk said, pursing his lips.

"This is bullshit!" Kyun snapped. "How can you even consider it. She picks one."

"What does Holly want?" Dante asked, looking at me. "No one has asked you that."

I blinked. Two minutes ago, I was certain I wouldn't ever be able to be with any of them, and now this? I didn't even know what to think. My brain couldn't handle the thought process fast enough and I was fairly certain my feelings had short-circuited at this point.

Before I could answer, there was an urgent knock

on the door, which developed into a hammer. Jun opened it. Park Inhye was there looking completely frazzled. "Holly, why are you not answering your phone?"

I had to think about what she was asking me—the question seemed so normal compared to everything else. "It died," I told her. It had died last night and it had never occurred to me to charge it. "Why?"

"We have a problem and you all need to pack right now!" she cried, bursting into the apartment.

"What's wrong?" I asked, alarmed, though thankful to have something else to focus on.

"Your brother is an asshole."

"And the sky is blue, but I'm not about to have a meltdown over the color of the sky," I pointed out, curious as to what Sejin had done this time.

"I was going through the emails—there's another account that had been created that you hadn't been given access to—and I found one for a sponsorship deal with a hotel on Jeju Island."

"That's a bad thing?" I asked, thinking the opposite.

Inhye shook her head. "The sponsorship part is a brilliant opportunity for H3RO. The problem is that Sejin signed it. They're expecting you today for the next ten days for a photoshoot and some video commercials."

"Then we need to rearrange it," I said. "We have a schedule." And *this* situation to deal with.

"If you cancel or rearrange it then you—H3RO, not Atlantis—are going to get sued. You've only just made enough money for the legal fees. This will destroy H3RO," she told me. Then she pulled something out of her purse and thrust it at me: a transparent folder containing passports and tickets. "I'm working through rescheduling this week, and seeing if anything can be moved to Jeju, but you've got three hours to get to the airport to get on the flight out there, so you need to move quickly. I'll take care of as much as I can from here, but you need to go, Holly. Now."

"OK," Tae agreed. He looked around the room. "We'll finish our discussion later when we get to Jeju. Right now, we have cases to pack and a flight to catch."

Just like that, H3RO listened to their leader, running off to their rooms. I watched them go while Inhye handed over a stack of information, including the contract. She disappeared so I could get ready, promising there would be two minivans downstairs waiting for us in no more than ten minutes.

I watched her leave, then stared down at the pile of papers in my hands. It felt like everything was imploding in on me and yet the only thing I could think about was Jun's words: *Why can't she be with all of us?*

No, there would be time to think of that later.

There would be a very awkward and uncomfortable hour-long flight to think about this.

Right now, I had to make sure H3RO would get on the flight, before Sejin got his way and H3RO didn't exist anymore.

*Then* I would see if they could survive me too.

I hurried towards my own bedroom, quickly throwing things into my case and carry-on bag. I'd never been to Jeju Island before, and all I knew was that it was to the south and warm. Given how warm it was here in Seoul, I packed what I would normally wear for work. The only difference was that I remembered to pack my bikini. Just in case.

Ten minutes later, we were all heaving our cases into the back of the two minivans Inhye had booked for us. I was in the front seat with the driver. Nate, Jun, and Dante were in the back, so it wasn't as bad as it could have been if I had been in the other minivan, but the atmosphere in this minivan was still tense.

The journey was spent in silence. I had a feeling that the thoughts of the guys in the back were very similar to mine: all of them and me.

I knew I should look through the pack Inhye had given me. I should have been finding out how long we would be in Jeju, what H3RO were required to do, and what we were bumping back in Seoul to accomplish this. I could also have spent the time productively working out ways to murder my asshole half-brother in his sleep.

But no …

Instead, I was honestly considering if what Jun had suggested could even be possible.

Could I do that?

Could they do that?

Was this all just insanity?

And what would happen when everyone else found out?

It was bad enough when fans found out their idol was dating someone, but how would they react when they found out all of H3RO was dating. And not different girls, but the *same* girl.

This was insane, right?

Our minivan arrived at the airport before the other one, and we had already unloaded our cases by the time it pulled up. Somehow, despite the last-minute decision to do this, there were already fans waiting for us, armed with their cameras and phones. How they found this information out was staggering.

"Minhyuk," I called. "We need to check in, I'm sorry." He was busy talking to one of the fans—he was happy to do that with anyone.

He nodded at me, said goodbye, then joined the edge of the group as I led them into the airport, looking for our check-in desk. The fans followed, keeping a polite berth.

From their perspective, I doubted anyone would have been able to tell how dysfunctional this group really was right now, but I could see it in the smallest of movements. Tae and Kyun stayed to themselves, hidden beneath caps, masks and sunglasses. They didn't say a word to anyone, not even each other, but I could tell that they were relying on each other with silent support.

Dante was smiling and waving at the fans, and although the smiles to them were genuine, whenever he turned his attention to whatever H3RO was doing, I could see the smile was forced and strained. He was doing his best to make it look like nothing was wrong.

Nate and Jun were keeping close to me, like my own personal bodyguards. I wanted to tell them not to—that they were probably going to make things harder between themselves and the rest of H3RO, but there was no way I could tell them that—not in a place as public as this.

And Minhyuk … for the most part, Minhyuk was avoiding everyone. He loved spending time with the fans, and he continued to do that, but I could see, even when we had been waiting outside, that he was trying to avoid any form of conversation with us.

I gathered the boarding passes from the woman behind the check-in desk, making sure they matched with the passports, before handing them out. This group was a hot mess, and this time, it was completely my fault.

# 제2 장

# *H3RO*

## *Island*

With the hot and humid weather, the captain announced that the short flight was likely to be bumpy as we would be flying over thunderstorms all the way down to the south of South Korea. I'm not good on planes, especially not when there's turbulence. Any plans I had of reading the paperwork Inhye had given me were going straight out of the window. It might only be a short flight, but I was going to be spending all of it clutching at the seatbelt in the first-class seat.

Inhye had no idea of anything that was happening with H3RO and myself when she booked the tickets, nor of my fear of flying, and as a result, I was sat next to the window, beside Tae. I was too distracted with the flight to narrow down the waves of emotion he was sending in my direction, but it was definitely falling somewhere under the 'not happy' umbrella.

I closed my eyes, biting at my lip as I held onto the seatbelt during takeoff. The last thing I wanted to do was look out the window. I could feel us level off, but with the bumps, the captain announced the fasten seatbelt sign was going to be kept on and it would be unlikely there would be a refreshment service. When I heard Tae's seatbelt click open beside me, my hand shot over, grabbing his thigh. "Don't!" I hissed at him.

He looked at me, tilting his head, but he paused in getting up.

"The captain has just said it's too bumpy to turn off the fasten seatbelt sign," I told him.

"You don't like flying?" he asked.

I shook my head, just as the plane shook like it was a cocktail and James Bond was after his Martini. I clenched my fists as my stomach did cartwheels and squeezed my eyes closed again. I didn't open them until I realized Tae was prying my hands free from his leg. "Sorry," I muttered as I started to pull my hand back.

Tae held on.

"How did you manage on your flight from Chicago? That must be at least twelve hours, right?"

"Fourteen, and I have tranquilizers, and the weather wasn't this bad," I told him. "We were in too much of a rush and I was a little distracted. I didn't bring them with me."

"Do you feel sick?" he asked me, hesitantly.

I shook my head. "It's not travel sickness." The plane lurched again. I clutched at Tae's hand, trying to convince myself that millions of people flew every day and nothing happened to them. Even though the rational part of my mind knew that was true, the part which was controlling my fear was laughing at me reminding me that we were in a giant metal box with wings, and were humans supposed to fly, they would have been born with wings. "It's up and then down," I whispered more to myself than to Tae.

"Up and down?" he repeated, hearing me.

"The flight," I explained. "It's about an hour, which means we go up and then we head back down. It's not like we have to stay up here for long."

"That's … interesting logic," he responded. I could almost hear the smile in his voice.

"It's my logic which is making me feel better."

If I wasn't strapped in, I would have jumped out of my seat when Tae's fingers touched my throat. My eyes shot open and I lurched back from him. "What are you doing?"

"You look like you're going to pass out," Tae said, watching me with his serious eyes. Because of the cast on his other arm, the motion had twisted him in his seat so he was facing me, and I didn't miss the fact he still wasn't wearing his seatbelt.

"I'm fine," I lied.

Tae pushed his fingers back on my neck, right on my neck. "No, I think you're about to pass out," he disagreed. I wasn't surprised. I was aware my pulse was racing.

"I'm not sure that's because of the plane," I muttered.

His eyes fixed on mine. Of all of H3RO, he had the most intense of gazes, and was often referred to as the stern member. I'd thought the same at first, then I realized that most of the time, that gaze was observing everything. Although not the most vocal, he was a leader who always knew where his members were and what they were doing.

Or, until recently he was.

He'd had no clue about what I had been doing with the others.

In an almost subconscious action, my body released some of its tension, but not for the right reason. Those dark eyes of his were ringed with betrayal and it wasn't all aimed at me. I reached up and pulled his hand down. "You have every right to feel angry, betrayed, disappointed—everything with me, but please don't think that of the others," I whispered. "They didn't know."

Tae's expression went blank, then he pulled his hand free and stood. Ignoring my protests, he moved down the aisle. Moments later, Minhyuk slipped into the seat next to me, looking both confused and concerned. "What just happened?"

"I—" I didn't get a chance to finish the sentence as the plane gave another lurch, bouncing up and down like it was going to drop from the sky. I let out a stream of expletives in both Korean and English, before leaning over to fasten Minhyuk's belt for him.

Recognition illuminated Minhyuk's eyes and he gave me a reassuring smile as he reached up and turned my air vent on. It was only when he started unravelling headphones that I realized he had taken the seat with something in his hands: Tae's old iPod. "Close your eyes, imagine you're on one of those rodeo bulls, and listen to the music."

"A rodeo bull?" I asked, snorting.

Minhyuk grinned. "Have you ever been on one?"

I slowly nodded, then stilled my head as he put an ear bud in my far ear. "I don't see the relevance."

"They're hilarious," he said, as though that explained everything. "And they're even more hilarious when you watch Jun on them."

"Do you want me to imagine me on it, or Jun on

it?" I asked, growing even more confused.

He shrugged. "Either." He scrolled through the iPod, settling on something. "Ten songs."

"Ten has a solo album?" I asked, wondering if the air vent was blowing out some form of drugged air, for all the sense Minhyuk was making. What did NCT's Ten have to do with anything?

"The number: listen to ten songs," he glanced down at the iPod, "Though there is some NCT-U on there."

"This makes no sense," I sighed as Minhyuk hit play and Monsta X burst into my ear.

"There seem to be a lot of things that don't make sense these days," Minhyuk said, giving me a wry smile. "Just think about rodeo bulls and listen to the music."

Rodeo bulls and Dramarama made for a bizarre combination.

Minhyuk pushed the second earbud into my other ear and I settled back into the chair, trying to imagine being on a rodeo bull. I had just about conjured up the image when the song switched over to Red Velvet's Ice Cream Cake and I had to giggle. I wasn't sure if I was more amused that I was listening to Red Velvet and thinking of riding a rodeo bull, or that Tae had the song on his iPod: he hated having to do girl group dances.

The next thing I knew, Minhyuk was gently tapping me on the shoulder. I pulled an earbud out as I gave him a questioning look. "I need to turn it off for landing."

My eyes went wide. "Already?"

"Distraction," he said, giving me a small smile. "Doesn't work for everyone, and it wouldn't have worked on a longer flight."

"How do you know this?" I asked, pulling the other earbud out and handing them back to Minhyuk.

"My parents used to travel a lot when I was younger. I didn't like flying."

"And that's what works for you?" I asked in disbelief.

Minhyuk shook his head. "The more I fly, the easier it gets."

"I hope so," I muttered as the plane wobbled.

The landing was smoother than the rest of the flight, and we were soon on the ground, taxiing to our gate. The next problem came with immigration. As Nate, Dante and I had non-Korean passports, we had a much longer line to stand in. Seeing as neither Nate or Dante seemed in a talkative mood, and I could hardly blame them for that, I finally pulled out the pack Inhye had given me.

I started with the contract.

Sejin was an asshole.

I wasn't sure who had drafted it, but even without a law degree, even I could see the terms were beyond unreasonable. I was surprised that the Atlantis Entertainment lawyers had even allowed this to be signed, which had me doubting that they'd ever seen it at all.

The work laid out wasn't unreasonable: two photoshoots and a commercial for the hotel resort, as Inhye had mentioned. All in all, it meant we would be staying here a full ten days. H3RO's payment for all this, was more than generous.

What I didn't like was the fact that if they broke the contract, then H3RO would be held personally responsible, and not Atlantis Entertainment, to the tune of 45 million won, *each*: if one person broke it, they were all accountable. I knew full well that none of the members would go out of their way to break that contract, but if it was them being personally accountable, then they should have signed it, and not Sejin. *Especially* considering we weren't even told about it. If it wasn't for Inhye, we would have broken this contract already and I was willing to bet it was ironclad enough that ignorance wouldn't help us in court.

Inhye was getting every single one of those benefits she had asked for. I would see to that!

I was also close to putting out a contract on my half-brother. I only stopped myself because that would be an easy way out for him.

Tae, Kyun, Minhyuk and Jun were waiting for us on the other side, huddled together in a corner. I frowned: we had left so last minute that we hadn't brought anyone else with us. I could understand why they had chosen to wait where they had, by immigration, as fans couldn't get near them. I had to cross my fingers that the crowd wouldn't be too big on the other side.

With the awkward silence still settled firmly over us, we went out to baggage claim. There was still a reasonable crowd around the carousel, but bags were still coming out. On the plus side, although they were getting a few looks, we were left to ourselves.

After twenty minutes of waiting, and the crowds around us thinning out, it was becoming very evident that we had another problem. "I've seen that case six times now," Minhyuk muttered.

"At least you've got your case," Jun grumbled, folding his arms as he stared sullenly at the carousel.

"Well, if you'd have grabbed your own instead of

mine, you'd have yours now," Nate was quick to point out.

"Technically, that's mine," Jun said, pointing at the silver case beside Nate.

"Like I said, you're the one who grabbed mine and insisted on swapping the tags over instead of putting your clothes into your own case," Nate declared. "It might have your stickers on it, but it sure as hell has my name on it and my things in it."

My suitcase and Jun's suitcase were the two we were waiting for. In the rush to get out of the door, Jun hadn't been paying too much attention to the nearly identical suitcases and had packed all of his things in the one of Nate's.

"It's not on this flight," I grumbled, admitting defeat. I reached over and tugged Jun's passport from his hands. "You guys wait here. I'm going to go file a report with the lost baggage people."

While I stood in a small line of people who had also lost their luggage, I pulled out my phone and called Inhye. "You got there?"

I nodded, even though she couldn't see me. "My brother needs a smack in the face with a truck," I snorted. "I'm willing to bet my liver that he did that intentionally."

"I think you're right," Inhye agreed. "But I don't think we would be able to prove it."

"Sadly not," I said, glancing back at the others. "But we have a few more problems," I told her. "I need a team. This contract has us doing a performance at the end of next week. We have no stylists, no outfits, and I'm learning very quickly why an idol group needs a small team of people with them."

"Don't worry, I have a plane booked for myself the day after tomorrow," Inhye quickly assured me. "I've already spoken to Jae and he's prepared to join you all and be your stylist, and, I'm just waiting for Ahn Soomi to confirm."

"Soomi?" I repeated in confusion. Ahn Soomi was the exceptionally talented woman who had directed and produced H3RO's comeback music video.

"I hope you don't mind, but I had an idea," Inhye apologized before quickly explaining. By the end of her explanation, I was grinning.

After a very long argument with the lost baggage desk, I returned to the group. They had moved to the side, out of the way of everyone, and were using their cases as seats. "The good news is that the two cases made it to Jeju," I said, with false cheer.

"They have no idea where they are, do they?" Jun sighed.

I nodded. "Their theory is that it got off the plane, where it was checked in with the airport, and then it ended up on the wrong carousel, or some form of nonsense like that."

"Which means I have no clothes?" Jun asked. He then rolled his eyes. "Why couldn't Dante's case go missing? He *likes* being naked."

Before I could stop myself, I looked over at Dante. He smirked. I cleared my throat and started turning. "They're going to find them and deliver them to the hotel, which is where we need to go," I declared, quickly leading them away from the baggage claim and out into the arrivals lounge.

Yet again, somehow, H3RO's fans were waiting for them. It was only a small amount, but it was an amount nonetheless. I had no idea where they got this information from. I would have to ask Inhye if there was a chance someone was leaking this information.

Thankfully, the hotel had sent a limo to pick us up, and we were soon safely taken to the beach resort. What I hadn't expected was that we were given our own villa within the resort. The bags were taken in for us, and a welcome spread had been laid out for us. This place was a palace and made the Atlantis retreat look like a hostel by comparison.

I was so busy with the flower display in the living room, that I didn't notice that Minhyuk had left the group and returned until he spoke up. "There's only six rooms."

# 제3 장
# H3RO

*Jealousy*

I glanced over at him, feeling the knot in my stomach make a reappearance. "So, go pick one," I said, quickly, keeping my tone. I picked up my purse with a smile. "Inhye, Jae, and a few others will be joining us in a few days, so I'm sure there's some more rooms booked for us."

Hoping to get out of there before the atmosphere plummeted again, I darted for the door. Even though the outside was even more humid than it had been in Seoul, it was still easier to breathe than it was inside. The resort was bigger than I thought, and the villas were to the far side of the main reception, at a more private section of the grounds.

I rounded a corner and paused, catching a glimpse of the ocean. I wanted to go and swim in that later, if the opportunity arose. "If I get my bikini by then," I muttered aloud.

"We could always go skinny dipping."

I whirled and shot Jun an unimpressed look. "Really?"

"It got in the way last time, anyway," he shrugged.

I sucked in a deep breath, and let it out in one long sigh. "Jun," I started.

Jun shook his head at me. "I'm missing my case," he said, as though that was the next natural thing to say. I arched an eyebrow at him. "The resort has a small mall," he continued. "I read it in the welcome guide."

"Jun," I started again.

Once more he cut me off. "I mean, I could walk around naked if you prefer. And you're more than welcome to join me." He gave me a look which had me feeling like my clothes had disappeared anyway. "But I need a toothbrush."

"You're telling me there's no toothbrush in the bathrooms?" I asked, my voice laced in skepticism.

"Dunno," Jun shrugged, slipping his hand into mine. "I never looked."

"Jun!" I cried, trying to pull my hand free. He held on. "We can't do this."

"Get an extra toothbrush?"

I held up our hands. "This."

Jun moved in front of me, tilting his head as he stared down at me. Then he smiled. "Come with me," he declared, tugging me towards a path that was leading towards the beach.

"Jun!" I objected. Jun didn't let go, leading me down a winding path until we eventually hit the sand. We took a few steps before I had to stop him. He turned to look at me and I rolled my eyes. "I came, didn't I?" I asked him. I pointed down at my feet. "I just want to take my shoes off before they fill with sand," I explained as I toed them off.

Jun immediately let go of my hand and stepped back while I crouched down to scoop my shoes up. I stood, but this time, Jun didn't take my hand. I think he had realized I wasn't going to run off. I still wanted to— I wanted to put off this conversation for as long as possible.

I walked past him, following the sand, hot beneath my bare feet, to the water, going just deep enough for the water to lap over the tops of my feet. Moments later, Jun was by my side, staring out to sea with me. "This place is like a tropical paradise," I muttered.

I closed my eyes, lifting my face to the open sea and the warm sea breeze that was coming in from it. It gently tugged at my hair and skirt; I wished it was strong enough to take all my troubles from my shoulders. When I realized that wasn't going to happen, I let out a long sigh.

"I know you seem set on avoiding everything, but we really should talk," Jun said, softly.

"I know," I agreed. I opened my eyes and turned, finding him watching me. "I'm sorry."

"What for?" he asked.

"Lying to you: being with you and with everyone else," I muttered, feeling the shame burn through me as I said it.

"You know I'd worked it out, right?" he asked me, pulling a face.

"Worked what out?"

"What was happening with you and the others."

I chewed at my lip before shrugging at him. "I had my suspicion, but that doesn't make what I did any less wrong."

"I'm not going to speak for the others," Jun shrugged. "They're vocal enough to do that themselves, but for me, I see how you got here. I knew what was happening, and I had the opportunity to speak up. In some respects, this is as much on me."

I shook my head. "This isn't on you."

"Placing blame and going around in circles isn't going to fix this," Jun told me, firmly. He reached over, placing his hands on my shoulders. "What you need to think about is what you want."

"What I want is to not hurt anyone." I sighed. "Any more than I already have."

Jun gently shook his head. "No, just you. Be selfish, and honest, for a few minutes. What do you want?" He glanced out to sea before looking back at me. "And if that answer is one of the others, don't worry about saying that … but what do *you* want?"

I closed my eyes. I knew what I wanted. I just knew I couldn't have it. When I opened my eyes, I found Jun's brown eyes staring at me. A small smile crept over his face. "What?" I asked, warily.

"You have me on board," he said.

"Jun, you can't possibly—"

"Am I wrong?" he asked.

I glowered at him, folding my arms. "No," I pouted. "And it's highly annoying that you know that, but I just don't see how this can work. How could anyone be OK with that kind of arrangement?"

"That's what we're going to work on," Jun responded. He pulled me to him, wrapping his arms around me. "I think Nate's willing to give it a go, and I'm fairly certain Minhyuk and Dante could be convinced."

"Just not Tae and Kyun," I mumbled into his arm. My arms snaked around Jun's waist.

"One at a time," Jun muttered.

This was insane.

This was never going to work.

But, I admitted to myself, I really wanted it to.

## H3RO

I sat in front of the mirror, putting the finishing touches to my makeup. Inhye had booked another villa, but the hotel had misunderstood, thinking I wouldn't need it until when Inhye and the others arrived in a couple of days. When Jun and I had arrived back at the villa, Nate pointed out that Tae and Kyun were sharing a room, so for now, I had one to myself in the same building.

The doorbell rang and I set the lipstick down, tightening the belt to the dressing gown to hurry out to answer it. Despite the airport's promises, there were still no bags for Jun and me. The hotel had been brilliant about it, promising to send over a selection of clothes for us. They'd also agreed that as soon as the cases arrived, they would be forwarded on too. Then they'd announced that they would be delivering us a meal to the villa for us to enjoy that evening.

Minhyuk was already there, ushering a man with a rack of garment bags into the entrance. I joined him, just as he looked at me questioningly. "It's for tonight," I explained.

Minhyuk pointed into the large living area where six other racks were waiting. "Then what are they for?"

My mouth fell open, reading the small name tags on their ends. "I guess you all get clothes," I shrugged. Each rack held what had to be a week's worth of clothing options. Seeing as I didn't have anything else to wear, I was refusing to feel guilty about it. I carefully gathered the items up and took them up to my room, hanging them, still in the garment bags, in the large closet.

A few weren't clothes that I would normally wear, and there was a dress in there that was very clearly for a wedding, but I found a nice maxi dress to put on.

I grabbed my phone and left the room, but instead of heading downstairs, I went to Nate's bedroom. I had barely spoken to him since this morning, and all other things aside, he had been drugged and released from the hospital only hours ago. He opened the door, looking surprised to see me, but stepped aside to let me in.

"I wanted to make sure you were OK," I told him. "You were in the hospital last night and the doctor said you might still feel side effects." I chewed at my lip. "I'm not sure putting you on a plane was the best idea."

"I slept all afternoon," he said, nodding his head at the unmade bed behind him. "I still have no idea what happened last night," he added.

"Which the doctor said would be likely," I reminded him.

Nate strode over to me, his hands gently clasping my face as he tilted it into the light. "How much makeup did you have to put on to cover that up?"

"Not that much," I lied. It had been getting blacker over the course of the day. It had taken a lot of make up to hide it.

"I am so sorry," he muttered, his fingertips gently tracing over my cheek as he focused on the area he had hit.

"It wasn't like you were aiming for me."

Nate's gaze flicked to meet mine, and I could feel the guilt radiating from his look. "For her," he said. "I don't even remember her, but I'm not excusing the fact that, at that moment, I chose to be with her. Please forgive me."

"Of course I do," I assured him, not breaking my gaze.

Nate nodded, releasing my face. He stepped past me, then he stopped, whirled on the spot and pulled me to him. The sudden movement had me stumbling, but his strong arms caught me, pulling me upright. His lips found mine.

Despite his actions, his kiss was gentle. Soft and sensual like a tease, it had me making a whimper from the back of my throat. I could feel his smile before he pulled back, just enough to nip at my lower lip. My mouth parted open, and his tongue slid in. My fingers moved to his hips, using the belt loops to slide through and anchor him to me.

Nate's hand slid up my side, cupping my breast as our tongues met. The dress I was wearing was backless, which meant no bra. The tips of his thumbs caressed my already aching nipples, sending a shiver down my back, and a jolt of something straight to my core. *Holy hell*, I was so turned on right now. As I rubbed up against him, unable to stop myself as his hand gently massaged my breast, I discovered I wasn't the only one who was getting turned on.

My hands left his belt loops, sliding up and under his shirt. I had just managed to trace the outline of hips and that wonderful 'v' indentation, when both of his hands abruptly left my body, only to grip my hands as he stepped away, breathing heavily. "I think we all need to talk."

"I think you're right," I agreed.

The atmosphere was still tense when we made our way downstairs and outside to a sheltered area. Underneath an enormous parasol, a table had been set, complete with a tablecloth, and enough cutlery that I was certain the 'meal' the hotel was providing was a little more than burger and fries.

Already at the table were Dante and Tae, both drinking beer. From where I was standing, I could see both Minhyuk and Jun inside, watching over several waiting staff who were hurrying around in the small kitchen. Jun caught me watching and I gave him an unimpressed look, pointing at the staff.

Catching on, Jun tugged at Minhyuk's sleeve and pulled him outside to join us. "Stop hovering," I hissed at the pair as one of the wait staff hurried over to us.

"Would you care for drinks?" she asked, trying hard not to stare at Minhyuk.

I gave her a grateful smile. "I truly appreciate the trouble the resort has gone to for us tonight, but we're very tired. Please could you leave things for us to take care of?" The woman's eyes went wide in alarm and I sighed. "I will call your manager and tell him I authorized it," I added. She nodded, though still looked wary.

While she passed on the message to the staff inside—all looking as alarmed as she had—I called the hotel as promised. There was something about the way the manager responded, no matter how much I tried to assure him this was my decision, that had me thinking the staff were going to get into trouble. I was tempted to change my mind, but the elephant in the room needed addressing and having people around was asking for trouble.

I waited for everyone to disappear before trying to work out what was being served. I probably should have asked seeing as the best I could guess was it was some kind of Mexican dish. Thankfully, Minhyuk came to the rescue. While he busied himself getting things together, I made use of the small bar we had been left with, and made up a couple of pitchers of lime margaritas.

Finally, we were all seated around the table in an awkward silence. It was like the air right before a big storm: charged, prickly, and ready to explode.

To hell with it …

I poured myself a generous glass of margarita and took a large sip. I winced … I may have been a little liberal with the tequila. Oh well … I took another mouthful and looked at the faces at the table. "Where's Kyun?" I asked.

"He's not hungry," Tae said, shortly.

"Well, I am," Minhyuk declared, reaching for the dishes and serving us all like everything was sunshine and roses.

I just took another mouthful of my drink.

# 제4 장

# *H3RㅇO*

*What Is Love?*

lthough the food was good, I don't think anyone really enjoyed it. Eating was just a motion. In the end, maybe because of the liquid courage the margarita had provided, I bit the bullet. "I like you all," I announced, suddenly, causing everyone to stare at me. "No," I shook my head. "No, that's not right. I fell in love with you all. I didn't think it was possible, but I did—I have. I don't think I could choose between any of you, if I wanted to." I sat back into my seat and shrugged. "So, that's where I stand."

"You already know my feelings on it," Jun said. "I want to be with you and I don't mind if my hyungs do too."

"Do you really?" Minhyuk asked him, his expression pensive. "I have been thinking about this since you've said it, but I don't see how it could work?"

"Because you're over thinking it," Jun told him. "It's about sharing time, not sharing Holly. And trusting each other."

Minhyuk chased a tomato around his plate looking completely bewildered. "I still don't see how this works, but ..." he trailed off, looking at me from underneath his eyelashes. "I will try."

Dante looked between me and Jun and then shrugged. "Why not?"

"Holly already knows my answer to this," Nate responded.

"What about you?" Jun asked Tae. We all looked down the table to the silent leader.

He had a great poker face most of the time, but right now, it was completely unreadable. Until he looked to me. In that moment, I knew he wasn't sold. "If you can get Kyun to agree to this, I'm in." He got up from the table and disappeared into the villa.

"Maybe this isn't a good idea," I muttered, slumping back in my chair. "The last thing I want to do is cause problems between all of you."

Minhyuk shuffled his chair over against mine, then wrapped an arm around my shoulder. "Kyun is very ..."

"Stubborn?" Jun offered, cheekily, earning himself a backhand to his arm from Dante. "Ow!"

Dante shot him an unimpressed look. "Have some respect for your hyung."

"He's only a few weeks older than me," Jun grumbled.

"Private," Minhyuk spoke up, shooting them both silencing stares. "Kyun is very private. The only one he opens up to is Tae. It's always been that way."

"Minhyuk has a point. If anyone can win him around, it will be Tae," Nate agreed.

"And if anyone can win Tae around, it's Holly," Jun added.

I shook my head. "I don't know if I want to 'win

them around'," I told them. "It's not a game. I love both of them and I don't want any of them, or any of you, hurt over this."

"I didn't mean it like that," Jun said, looking surprised.

"I need to go to bed," Nate suddenly announced, making all four of us look at him.

"Are you OK?" I asked.

Nate nodded, getting to his feet. "I had little sleep last night, and I think I need to sleep the rest of what was in me off. I'm just tired." He assured me. He hovered there for a moment, then with a slight shrug, leaned over and kissed me. It wasn't a peck on the cheek either.

Minhyuk's arm around my shoulder didn't move. Maybe it was because I was drunk, but I kind of liked it.

"Night," Nate announced as he pulled away. He gave the guys a short salute, then walked into the villa.

The four of us sat there. I wasn't sure about the others, but I had no idea what to say to that.

It was Dante who moved first. He leaned forward, resting his forearms on his thighs with a loud sigh. Then he ran his hand over his face. "Yeah, this is going to take some getting used to," he muttered, before he too got to his feet and followed Nate inside.

Minhyuk rubbed my shoulder. I reached up and held his hand before standing up. When I started stacking the discarded plates in a pile, Jun shot to his feet. "I have to do a thing," he announced, then all but ran into the villa.

I turned to Minhyuk with an arched eyebrow. "He doesn't have a thing, does he?"

"He does," Minhyuk told me as a mischievous

grin spread over his face. "It's called avoiding his assigned chores."

"That doesn't surprise me anymore," I muttered, dryly. I carried the pile of plates into the kitchen and scraped what debris there was into the trash can before running the faucet. I quickly rinsed them then loaded them into the dishwasher.

Minhyuk appeared beside me with more dishes. He set them on the side with the others and then disappeared. Or I thought he had. The next thing I knew, his arms had slipped around me and his chin was resting on my shoulder. "Hi," he mumbled.

I paused to glance at him over my shoulder, then set the dish I had been holding down. "Hi," I returned, frowning slightly. Dante may have been vocal about it, but Minhyuk wasn't as sure about this situation either. "I know this whole thing is strange, to say the least, but don't do anything you're not comfortable with, Minhyuk," I told him gently.

"No, it's not that," he said, still mumbling into my shoulder. I started to turn so I could face him and speak to him properly, but his grip tightened, holding me in place.

"Is everything OK?" I asked, my hands settling gently on his.

He shook his head. "No … yes … no …"

I laced my fingers through his. "Whatever it is, you can tell me." His fingers tightened around mine. Minhyuk was possibly the most considerate member of H3RO, always looking out for the others in a different way to Tae. Fans had dubbed him the mother of the group, and it was easy to see why when he was always fussing after them and making sure everyone was happy.

So, I wasn't used to him being this shy. The only time I had really witnessed it was … when he was trying to be close to me …

"I'm worried," he admitted.

Maybe I was wrong.

"I know this is a really strange situation, but—"

"It's really not that," he said, cutting me off. "I mean, it is a strange situation, and I don't know if …" he exhaled, his breath hot against my neck. "I'm not … I've only had one girlfriend before," he blurted out. "And until now, I've honored the 'no relationships' clause in my contract."

Gently, but firmly, I pulled his arms tighter around me, then I turned my head, pressing my lips against his cheek. "I don't care about that," I told him.

"I don't have as much experience as the others."

"I don't care," I repeated.

He swallowed. "I don't want—"

"I don't care," I said, firmly, turning slightly in his arms. "It's not a competition, Minhyuk." I kept eye contact with him. For someone who was used to being on stage, he wasn't comfortable with it at all, but I needed him to understand what I was saying.

Realizing it wasn't working, I slowly swiveled in his arms and made the first move. He didn't stop me, but his kiss was hesitant. I pulled back, tilting my head. "Minhyuk," I said, softly. "If you're not comfortable with any of this, you don't have to do it."

It was like one of those cliched moments in a teen RomCom where the guy was telling the girl they didn't have to have sex if she wasn't ready, only this wasn't a movie, and the roles were reversed. A bolt of panic shot through me as Minhyuk stared at me, not responding.

I'd allowed myself to want it.

It was hard enough at the thought of Tae and Kyun never coming around to the idea, but Minhyuk too? That was soul crushing.

After what felt like an eternity, he nodded. "I just need to move at a slower speed," he said.

"Then you set the pace," I told him, simply. "I'll follow your lead."

I could feel Minhyuk relax against me and he leaned into me, kissing me gently. He was less hesitant this time, moving his mouth against mine. I could taste the biting tang of lime on his mouth, a sharp contrast to his soft lips. His hands slowly unraveled from around my body to settle on my hips, then he pulled away, smiling timidly.

I reached up to brush my hand through his hair. It had grown long again, and unstraightened, it was fluffy with a slight curl to it. "I love you," I murmured. My hand froze. OK, that wasn't a lie, but that was as far from taking it slow as I could get with our clothes still on. "I'm sorry," I quickly apologized. "That wasn't letting you set the pace."

Minhyuk's smile was shy. "I love you too," he said.

I breathed out a sigh of relief and relaxed into him, holding him tightly.

*Please let this work …*

## H3RO

The first thing on the schedule was a meeting with the resort owner, Hong Changseok. Inhye's notes weren't descriptive, but she had put down that he had requested

Tae go with me.

I sat at the breakfast bar drinking a very expensive tasting cup of coffee feeling nervous. When it came to my relationship with Tae, he'd been angry and hurt when he'd found out who my father was, and rebuilding that trust hadn't been easy. I was sure that the latest revelation hadn't just destroyed that again, but obliterated it.

The idea of spending time alone with him left me feeling uncomfortable because I was riddled with guilt. It was why I was only able to stomach a coffee and not eat breakfast.

I had asked Tae to come with me the night before, and he had agreed. Now I was questioning that.

Thankfully, he appeared: freshly showered and shaven, wearing what I guessed to be one of the outfits that had been brought over the night before as I hadn't seen it before. He was also sporting a somber expression. I bit back the sigh. Tae normally looked serious, and his beautiful wide and gummy smile was rare, but he was never normally this stern.

The resort had provided us with a couple of golf buggies so we wouldn't have to walk around the vast grounds if we didn't want to. Given H3RO's growing popularity, the trouble we'd been having with 'fans', and the simple fact a ride in awkward silence would be much quicker than a walk in awkward silence, we took the buggy.

I could sense that Tae wanted to drive, probably so he could keep his attention strictly on the path in front of us, however, he, like Nate, had been out of the hospital only a couple of day and his left arm had a cast around it. I took the driver's seat and he, thankfully, took the seat beside me, but kept his attention on the resort around us.

Even the tropical paradise wasn't a big enough distraction from the atmosphere on a buggy with no walls. "How is your arm?" I asked, searching for something to break the silence.

"Fine," he answered, shortly.

I puffed out my cheeks and looked back at the scenery, once again praying that I hadn't completely ruined things between us.

The main building oozed elegance. We walked through the familiar marble entrance I had been in the day before, following a lady to Hong Changseok's office. His office was as impressive as my father's, with the only difference being the amazing ocean view.

Hong Changseok seemed pleased to see us until he saw Tae's cast. "What is that?"

"There was an incident a few days ago, and unfortunately Tae broke his arm, but Tae is still able to fulfill his contractual obligations," I explained.

"You expect him to be able to do a photoshoot with a cast on his arm? We're doing this in partnership with a designer label *and* top sports brand," Hong Changseok pointed out. "This is an exclusive resort."

"Which is why you asked H3RO to be a part of it," I returned. "This group are professionals and will not let you down. I guarantee that you will not be able to tell," I added, ignoring the side-eye Tae was giving me.

Hong Changseok rested his elbows on his knees as he laced his fingers together. "Then let me ask you about Nate Choi and the bruise you're trying to hide on your face."

"I don't think that's any of your business." Tae was quick to jump in, surprising me. I turned to look at him, my head tilted slightly, but he ignored me. "It is rather rude to draw attention to a mark on a woman's face when she's trying to hide it with makeup."

Hong Changseok stared at Tae, then slowly nodded his head. "Yes, I supposed that is. My apologies, Miss Lee. However, seeing as I am asking this group to represent my brand, and ultimately, my name, I feel I am within my rights to ask about the behavior of one of its members, especially when that member had made papers for various inappropriate acts."

Shame and anger rippled through me. Shame from the fact that I had been so distracted about my love life that I hadn't thought to release a statement regarding the incident. Anger from the fact my asshole half-spawn was doing an appalling job, *again*, at protecting its employees. If I hadn't had that statement released, he should have done it. "Hong Changseok-*ssi*," I said, being exceptionally formal with the man. "Let me assure you that Nate Choi was trying to protect me that evening. Unfortunately, that woman who he was photographed with had drugged him, which is why his actions were clumsy. Nate, and the rest of H3RO, are one of the most sincere and professional groups I have ever met, and anyone who claims otherwise will be hit with a lawsuit for slander."

An approving smile spread over Hong Changseok's face as he nodded. "That is what I wanted to hear." He stood and walked over to his desk, picking up a photograph and walking over to hand it to me. Two awkward looking twin boys, each hiding behind a pair of thick glasses were staring at me. "These are my sons. It's their seventeenth birthday next weekend. It is their party that H3RO will be staying an extra night for, for a private performance. They're huge fans."

I blinked a couple of times—that was not what I was expecting to hear. I had assumed it would be a more public event where fans would have the opportunity to attend. I had a feeling a private performance would only upset the fans. "I will need to check our schedules," I replied, frowning.

"It was already agreed with Lee Sejin," Hong Changseok, told me. "Your schedule was organized around this."

"Of course," I agreed, not wanting to upset him.

We finished up soon after and made our way back to the lobby. It was a strange meeting, but once again, I found myself raging at my asshole half-brother. Not only had he not told us about this whole ten-day excursion *or* the terms if we failed to meet it, but he had been banking on that. Those two boys could have been very disappointed and that wasn't their fault.

Tae had gone back to walking in silence, which didn't surprise me. Then again, I was busy emailing Inhye. Which was when an uneasy feeling settled over me. I stopped and looked around, trying to work out what it was. My eyes fell on a family in the seating area. Two teenage girls had spotted Tae and were pointing excitedly.

I slipped my phone back into my pocket, ready to pick up my pace so we could get back to the villa, when one of the hotel employees came hurrying over to me. "Your suitcases have arrived," he explained after bowing in greeting. "Please allow me to have someone take them and you back to your villa."

Tae was now taking selfies with the two girls, so I nodded. I walked over to Tae. He didn't seem bothered by it, so I waited patiently for them. Finally, Tae gave them both a respectful smile and gestured to me. "That is my manager. I must leave," he told them apologetically, then flashed them his beautiful gummy smile. The girls ran back to their parents, shrieking excitedly.

Tae turned to me, the smile vanishing. "Mine and Jun's cases have arrived, so they're going to run us back to the villa," I explained.

We were taken outside where our golf buggy was waiting for us. The employee was busy loading my case onto the back of it beside Jun's, pulling a face as he did so. I pursed my lips: it wasn't *that* heavy. He then hurried around to the driver's seat, as Tae and I got on behind him.

With the sun now higher in the cloudless sky, the resort looked different again. It was going to be a scorcher today. The sea looked especially inviting, and I was glad that my case had turned up as my bikini was in it. I sucked in a deep breath, then wrinkled my nose. Something in the air didn't smell pleasant.

# 제5 장

# *H3R오*

*Will You Be Alright?*

The others were in the kitchen when we arrived back. Minhyuk had been cooking again as they were sat around the breakfast bar eating. When Jun saw his case being wheeled in behind us, he let out a whoop of joy and charged over, taking it and mine from the hotel staff, and pulling it over to the large sitting area.

"Did everything go OK?" Minhyuk asked, hurrying over to pour me a fresh cup of coffee.

I took it from him with a nod. "We were asked if we could return for a private performance." I started to explain. "A birthday party."

Then, from the other side of the room, Jun let out a cry. "Where's all my underwear?"

All six of us stopped and turned to stare at Jun in astonishment. "Are you sure you packed them?" Dante asked, smirking.

Jun rolled his eyes. "They're always the first thing I put in."

Minhyuk wandered over and pulled a face. "That case is as chaotic as your room. I'm surprised you can tell."

"Nate saw me pack! It was not this untidy, was it, *hyung*?"

Nate gave a nonchalant shrug. "I couldn't tell from over the piles of clothes on your side of the room."

"Nate!" Jun whined. "Tell them!"

Nate joined Minhyuk's side and frowned at Jun's case. "OK, it wasn't that bad. But are you sure that you really did pack them? Are we going to get back and find them buried under your blankets?"

"I packed my underwear!" Jun cried, indignantly. He folded his arms in a huff.

With a sigh, I set my coffee down and walked over, peering into the mess that was Jun's case. "Are you sure they're not in there?" I asked, calmly.

Jun shook his head. "They're not in there."

"Maybe the airport did a security check on the cases?" I suggested. "If they were sat around, they might have needed to check them."

"What about your case?" Jun asked. He picked it up, then pulled a face, wrinkling up his nose.

"It's not that heavy," I muttered.

"It smells," he informed me.

I pulled my own face of confusion as I walked around to his side of the couch. Had one of my bottles of perfume broken? "Airport security *must* have been through them: mine's missing its lock," I pointed out in irritation as I crouched down in front of it. That wasn't the first time I'd collected a bag where the supposedly airport security approved lock had been removed.

I unzipped the bag, pulled the lid open … and was assaulted by a horrific smell which had me falling backwards, covering my nose and mouth and fighting back the urge to throw up.

"What the hell is that?" I heard Kyun cry from the other side of the kitchen. "Get it out of here!"

Dante moved first, slamming the case closed, scooping it up, and carrying it outside. We all followed him, keeping a safe distance as we held our noses. It was Minhyuk who was brave enough to open it again, releasing the smell. It was like something had crawled into my case and died.

Tentatively, he prodded in it, picking up an item of clothing. I would have died in embarrassment at the sight of him holding a bra in the air, if it wasn't for the fact it had been shredded and was covered in something thick and gooey, giving the white fabric a greenish sheen. "Rotten eggs," he declared, dropping the bra so he could close the case.

"What the hell?" I said, feeling faint. I hadn't put eggs in there when I'd packed it.

"Minhyuk, is anything salvageable?" Tae asked.

"I think most things will be washable, but I'd want to clean everything before I touched it to—"

"Just throw it away," I said, with a shudder. I hadn't brought anything that couldn't be replaced and I didn't want that thing anywhere near me.

"Dante, take it out front," Tae instructed him. "I will get the hotel to dispose of it." He paused, then turned to me. "Are you OK?" he asked, gently.

I nodded, feeling numb. Why the hell would anyone do that? I watched Dante disappear around the side of the villa with the case, then narrowed my eyes. "Jun, what else is missing from your case?" I asked, a little sharper than was necessary.

Jun's eyes widened, surprised at my tone, but he shook his head. "I don't know. Let me check." He disappeared back into the villa.

"Tae, do not call the hotel just yet. I'm going to the police," I announced. I felt sick, and not just because of the lingering smell.

"I thought airport security was supposed to be some of the strictest in the world," Minhyuk muttered.

"This was nothing to do with the airport," Tae disagreed. "This was someone taking the bags from the baggage claim while we were held up in Immigration."

"Then I am definitely going to the police," I told them.

"I will come with you," Tae declared.

I shook my head. "You will stay here with the others. We don't need any of you being photographed at a police station." I walked back into the villa to retrieve my phone from where I had set it down beside my coffee, but stopped when Jun stepped outside. "Did you …?" I trailed off.

"Did you call the police already?" he asked, nodding his head at the two men behind him.

I slowly shook my head while giving the two gentlemen an expectant look. "We're here from the Jeju Police, but we're working in conjunction with Gangnam Police. We'd like to speak to you and Nate Choi about an incident in Seoul a couple of nights ago, on their behalf."

"Are we under arrest?" I asked, surprised at how calm I sounded, considering my heart felt like it was about to explode.

"No, but we would like to ask you some questions."

"If it's all the same with you, I would request that myself and Nate came to the police station tomorrow. Seeing as both Nate and I are American citizens, I would like to have my company's legal representation with us, to make sure we are understanding everything correctly."

The two men looked at each other, then one nodded, handing over a card. "Please see to it you come before lunchtime."

I waited for them to leave, then hurried over to the breakfast bar, doing little more than sparing a glance at Dante who had returned and was washing his hands. I ignored the questions that were flying around and instead, I dialed Inhye's number.

"Holly!" Nate exclaimed, looking terrified.

"Just a second," I said to him as Inhye answered. "Inhye, I need you down here sooner than tomorrow."

"I can be out on the next flight," she said, without even questioning it.

"I also need you to bring a lawyer with you."

There was a moment of silence. "Holly, what happened?"

"I don't think it's anything to be too concerned about," I said, fixing my eyes on Nate as I said it. "But I would like an expert down here because I'm barely familiar with the American legal system, never mind the Korean one. Plus, I want to know exactly what we have to do to get a restraining order on a crazy bitch, as well as suing her."

Six mouths simultaneously dropped open.

"Give me an hour to arrange this," Inhye said before she hung up.

"Are you serious?" Kyun asked, eyeing me with

suspicion.

I nodded. "I told you once that I wasn't going to let anyone hurt this group anymore. I don't care if it's one member or all of you. I am not putting up with this crap any longer, and, on behalf of Atlantis Entertainment, I'm sorry you've had to, and I'm sorry no one has done anything before now."

## H3RO

I spent most of the afternoon alone in my room on my phone. I had to get some work done anyway, given what had happened over the last few days, namely a statement which I was going to get the lawyer to check over. I'd told the guys to go out and enjoy the resort. "But if you're working, so should we," Minhyuk protested.

I handed him the iPad. "Fine, go do a V Live."

I wasn't surprised when Jun took the device, wrapping his arm around Minhyuk's neck, and pulling him away. "Come on!" he cried. "We can throw Dante in the ocean then video him taking his shirt off."

Dante smacked the back of his head.

"Fine," Jun said, rubbing the spot he'd been hit. "We'll throw Nate in—"

Dante charged at Jun, tossing him over his shoulder, then charged out the door, yelling, "Start filming!"

I was grateful when the others ran after him. It wasn't so much that I wanted them to leave, so much that I wanted them to distract each other for a few hours.

I was almost done with the statement when I heard Inhye's voice calling through the villa. I set the pen down and then hurried down to the kitchen where Inhye and a man were standing.

"I am so glad to see you," I told her.

"The rest of the team is still coming tomorrow," she said, apologetically. "It was too short notice for a lot of them. We've also not been able to check into this resort, so we're staying a couple of kilometers down the road at the sister resort, which is why we are slightly delayed."

"Inhye, you both dropped everything to get out here. I am exceptionally grateful for that." I turned to the man and held my hand out. "Thank you for coming. I'm Holly Lee, H3RO's manager."

The man gave me a dazzling smile, and if Inhye had told me he was just an actor playing a lawyer, I would have believed her. He was gorgeous. He was also older than both me and Inhye (although closer in age to Inhye), and I suddenly remembered that this was Korea and shaking hands was not the way to do things. Before I could drop my hand, he reached out and grabbed it, shaking it firmly. "I am Byun Yongdae," he said. "Lee Woojin has already informed me that I am to answer to you in his stead."

I caught the look of surprise from Inhye out of the corner of my eye, but was too busy hiding my own to acknowledge it.

"Your father has briefed me on the situation at Atlantis," he continued.

"Then I guess I should brief you on the situation here," I said, leading them over to the lounge so we could talk comfortably. I spent the next couple of hours briefing them on everything that I knew. We'd just come up with a game plan when H3RO arrived back from the beach. Their bright spirits evaporated the moment they saw us.

"OK, there's no need for faces like that," I told them. "We have good news, which includes issuing a statement that Atlantis Entertainment will be taking strong legal action against any malicious rumors, false statements, and personal attacks that are being spread online which defame H3RO or Atlantis." I looked to Yongdae. "I got that right, didn't I?"

Yongdae nodded. "Exactly correct." He turned to H3RO. "I am the lawyer that has been assigned to this, and I want to assure you that I will be taking every threat and comment seriously. Your manager had done the right thing by bringing me in, so if you come across anything which makes you feel uncomfortable, let her know and she will in turn, report it to me."

"Thank you," Tae said, bowing his head at Yongdae. I caught the look of relief in his eyes. I also didn't miss how Kyun sought out his hand, even though his face remained expressionless. This should have been done sooner.

Nate cleared his throat. "What about me?" he asked, rubbing at the back of his neck.

"I have heard Holly's take on things, and I wish to speak to you privately later, but tomorrow shouldn't leave you feeling concerned. I spoke to my colleagues in Seoul who have spoken to the detectives there. It seems some members of the public were concerned with you hitting Holly and reported it. Unless Holly wishes to press charges, we should be able to clear this up quickly. I have already been assured that my colleagues are also visiting the club to collect CCTV evidence."

I could see Nate visibly sag in relief and I had to

fight back the urge to hurry over to his side. Thankfully, Minhyuk did the job for me, wrapping an arm around his waist, while Dante leaned over and clamped his hand on Minhyuk's shoulder. "I told you that you had nothing to worry about."

"I think this is a good time to wrap things up," I said to Inhye and Yongdae.

"I will make sure this statement is released tonight," Inhye said with a small smile. She was also a fan of H3RO, so I knew she was happy they were being looked after. "Then we can go for dinner."

I shook my head. "H3RO have their shoot tomorrow, remember? I ordered food to be delivered for us, then we're getting an early night."

"Oh," Inhye muttered. "OK."

"But I also booked a table at the restaurant at this resort for you and Yongdae," I assured her.

Her eyes went wide. "Just us?" she squeaked, turning red as she refused to look in Yongdae's direction.

*Holy hell*, Inhye had a crush on Yongdae. "Yes," I said firmly. "I shall join you next time, but you two should go relax. Think of it as a thank you for dropping everything to come out here." I glanced to Yongdae. "Is that OK with you?"

Yongdae gave Inhye a look which she missed, but I certainly did not. "That sounds wonderful."

Inhye was single, and I hadn't seen a wedding band on Yongdae's finger. Maybe this would be a good thing.

# 제6 장

# H3RⓄ

*Killing Me*

The resort had sent over another meal, though I opted to eat it in my room. I was busy pouring over the comments that had been left on the group's Instagram posts, which, thanks to Jun who loved to post everything, was a lot. I was taking a screen shot of everything, while composing a list to see who were repeat offenders.

I did have an early night though. Although Jae and the crew would be getting in around lunch time, the photoshoot for the resort would be using their own crew. Or, at least the photographer and stylists they had hired for the advertisement campaign. We weren't escaping an early role call—I wasn't sure of their concept, but given the timing, I had a feeling the sunrise would be involved.

For some reason I couldn't get to sleep. I puffed out a breath and reached for my iPad, hoping that watching a few episodes of something would send me off. I settled into the first episode of 'Strong Woman Do Bong Soon'. When I was already chuckling, I suspected I would be watching a few episodes before sleep won out.

There was a light rap at the door, and at first, I thought I was imagining things. I paused the episode, listening. There was another rap. I pushed the iPad to the side and padded over to the door, opening and finding Nate there. "Is everything OK?" I asked in a whisper. He looked gaunt, with big bags under his eyes. Even his skin looked like it had taken on a grayish hue.

"Can I come in?" he whispered back.

I nodded, stepping aside. I closed the door behind him. As soon as I turned back to him, I was enveloped in a bearhug. I hugged him back. "What's wrong?"

"Can I stay with you tonight?" he asked, quietly. I pulled back and peered up at him, just as the light from the iPad turned itself off. "Was I interrupting something?"

"I couldn't sleep," I explained, leading him over to the bed where I switched the lamp on. I plucked the iPad from the bed, then set it on the cabinet. I quickly rearranged the pillows so I wasn't hogging them all, then got in, shuffling across to the far side. Nate got in beside me.

Once settled, he turned on his side, bringing his elbow up under his cheek. "What were you watching?"

"A drama," I settled into the bed, mimicking his pose. "What's up?"

"I can't sleep either," he admitted, following it up with a deep sigh. "There's something I need to tell you." He paused, then reached out for my cheek, gently brushing his fingers over the top of the bruise. I'd washed my makeup off before getting into bed, so the bruise was prominent. "I really am sorry about that."

I reached up, taking his hand in mine, and settling

it between the two of us. "I know, but I don't hold you at fault for that."

Nate slowly nodded. "That's not what I needed to tell you though."

"OK," I said, patiently.

He rearranged our hands so his was holding mine. "I am scared about tomorrow," he admitted.

I gave him a reassuring smile. "We've got our lawyer here," I told him. "You don't need to be worried about that."

"Not that part," he said, looking away. "That … that wasn't my first fight."

"I heard," I shrugged.

"After the last one, Lee Sejin told me that if there were any more, he was going to see to it that my contract was voided."

I pulled my hand free and rolled over so I could sit upright. "Nate, what you did was hardly a fight."

"No, but it was an act of violence, even if I did it with good intentions. And that girl was saying I was all over her. What if she changes her story and says she didn't want it."

"She would be an idiot changing her story and no one would believe her," I shrugged.

"Wouldn't they?" Nate asked as he sat up, crossing his legs beneath him. "Look at what happened to SHINee's Onew: he got drunk, accidentally touched a girl when he stumbled, and even though she admitted it was probably an accident, it was still pushed forward to prosecution."

"Which was dismissed," I pointed out.

"After nearly a year," Nate returned. "And H3RO's not SHINee, and I'm not Onew. I haven't been charged before, but I have been fighting before. My record isn't exactly great."

I reached over, taking both of his hands in mine. "The person you hit was me. I am not pressing charges. That girl spiked your drink, and you have me and Atlantis behind you, like Onew had his company."

"But do I?" he asked. "Have Atlantis' backing?" he clarified when I pulled a face. "Because look what's happening with Hyunseo and Bright Boys."

Bright Boys was the younger group my other half-brother, Seungjin, was in. He had spoken to me recently about saving them, but I had been so busy with everything that was happening with H3RO, that I hadn't done anything. In all honesty, I had very little knowledge of what had happened with that group. "I don't know what's happened with Bright Boys," I admitted. "But if it's something which could lead to the group being disbanded, and not just one of them being punished, then it's probably a little more complicated than what's happening with you."

"I don't know the details, but I do know there's more to it than there appears," Nate told me, chewing his lip.

"I'm your manager, not theirs," I pointed out. "I'm not sure I'm capable of doing anything to save them."

"I'm not asking you to," Nate sighed. "I just … Atlantis doesn't have their back, so why would they have mine?"

I squeezed his hands. "Nate, I have your back," I promised him. "And if it makes you feel better, I told Seungjin I was going to look into what's happening with Bright Boys."

I could see a small bit of tension leave Nate's body. I didn't think it would go completely until we returned from the police station. He leaned forward, pressing his forehead against mine. "I don't know how I managed without you," he whispered. "I love you."

"I love you," I told him. I tilted my head, bring my mouth up to meet his. I didn't realize until then, just how much.

I teased at his lips, but Nate pulled away with a sigh. "I can't, Holly. Not tonight. Even with you in front of me like this, I can't take my mind off tomorrow, and if I can't devote one hundred percent of my attention to you … I can't …"

I bent towards him and kissed his cheek. "OK."

Silently, Nate reclined back into the bed, pulling me with him. I rested my head on his chest, listening to his heart beat. "It's going to be OK, Nate," I promised him.

## H3RO

We didn't get much sleep. In the end, I had brought the iPad back into play and we stayed up watching a few more episodes of Strong Woman Do Bong Soon. I think, by the time the alarm went off, we had probably only had a couple of hours sleep.

Nate left my room to return to his and I showered, trying to wash away my exhaustion. It didn't work. When I entered the kitchen and found the rest of H3RO looking as tired as I did, I knew it was going to be a long day.

I moved over to the couch and shook Jun awake again. He'd moved from his bed to the couch to make it look like he was up. He looked up at me from under his hoodie with bleary eyes that were barely open, but followed me without any resistance outside to where a minibus was waiting for us.

It was a short drive down to the beach. The minibus took us part way onto the sand where a selection of gazebos was waiting for us. The sand was still damp beneath us and in the electric lights under the gazebos, I could see the sea on its way out.

There was a cold breeze coming in from the sea and I lifted my face to it, welcoming the salty air, even though it had me pulling my jacket tightly around me. While the guys got ready with hair and makeup, I waited for the photographer and shoot director to arrive to discuss the finer points of the week.

They arrived a short time after us and joined me. The assistant handed over a stapled pile of papers. I leafed through them while they explained the plans: it was going to be a long week.

Lee Sejin had signed H3RO up for a sponsorship which paid exceptionally well, but would have them working hard. There was a sunrise and sunset shoot almost every day from various points around the resort, including a private island I didn't even know existed (that one involved an even earlier morning). There were two sports clothing spreads, utilizing the various facilities the resort had. There were also three spreads for a top line designer. On top of all the group shots, there were individual shots. And as if that wasn't enough, there were individual shots for both clothing lines.

I puffed out my cheeks as I read it through. They could do it—I didn't doubt that. But I did wonder if

Inhye's special project involving Soomi was going to happen. The only time we would have for it would be at the weekend—before our flight back to Seoul—unless we could multi-task on a shoot. Given that half of H3RO were not firing at one hundred percent, if they wanted to rest, I was going to axe those plans.

A chair was brought over to me, and I settled into it, pulling out my phone. I'd noticed emails from both Inhye and Yongdae when I'd gotten up, but hadn't had a chance to read them.

I was lost in my inbox by the time the guys were ready for the first shot. Honestly, smart phones were a curse. It was only glancing up to rest my eyes that I spotted Dante walk out from the gazebo in a navy-blue suit. *Holy Hell!* He looked just as good in this as he had modeling underwear.

One by one, they all emerged, all looking as equally as handsome as each other. I won't lie: I sat and stared.

I knew these guys, and I couldn't pick a favorite, but as even as an outsider, I had to wonder how anyone ever picked a bias?

By the time the sun had risen the group shoot was wrapping up. I was joined by Inhye who looked like she hadn't had much sleep at all, and Yongdae, who didn't look much better. I arched an eyebrow at her. "You didn't need to come this early," I told her as my attention was caught by the smell of food. Caterers from the hotel had also arrived and were unloading a breakfast spread.

"That was my doing," Yongdae said apologetically. "The police station is over an hour away. I wanted us to arrive at a reasonable time. Inhye also received the schedule this morning and noted that if we arranged for Nate to do his solo shots first, we could go to the station and be back without worrying about the evening shoot."

I had to bite my lip to stop me from grinning ear to ear. How on earth would Yongdae know that Inhye had received that email? Given how early it was, I had a feeling there was a very simple explanation for that … "I'll go speak to the photographer now." I started to walk away, and then paused, turning back to Yongdae. "I feel rude asking, but would you mind not waiting around the set? I'm not going to tell Nate until he's done. I want him to be able to focus on the shoot without worrying."

Yongdae nodded. "Of course."

I glanced at Inhye, once again keeping my face straight. "You can go with him if you need to?"

"I'll stay," she said, quickly. "I have things to discuss with you and if I'm going to be here instead of you while you're with the police, I may as well stay here now, and then you won't have to hand things over to me."

I went over to the photographer and made my request without sharing the details. He didn't seem to care and agreed, sending his assistant to make sure Nate was ready first. When I returned to Inhye, Yongdae had already left.

"We didn't sleep with each other," she blurted out.

I held my hands up. "I will admit, I thought there was something there between you, but I wasn't going to ask."

"There is," she sighed, hanging her head. "It's just

complicated."

I glanced back at the gazebos, catching glimpses of H3RO as stylists fawned around them. "Isn't it always?" I asked.

# 제7 장

# H3R으

*A Little Closer*

When we stepped out of the police station, and into the hot humid air of Jeju City, I had to keep myself from breathing a sigh of relief because Nate was standing next to me. It wasn't that I had doubted Yongdae, but I'd seen a few articles of various idols being arrested or questioned for things that would have most people back home rolling their eyes and saying "are they really arresting him over *that*?".

Yongdae turned to me. He looked pleased. I wanted to hug him, but also refrained from doing that too. "Unless you have further need for me, I will return to Seoul and see to it that things are closed out with the Gangnam police?"

I nodded. "Thank you very much for coming down on such short notice, Yongdae," I told him, shaking his hand. "And thank you for all your help."

"While it was a pleasure, I hope the next time I see you will not be under work related matters," he smiled.

"Stop by my office any time," I agreed.

I waited for Yongdae to get a taxi, and then

walked over to Nate who had drifted away from the police station at Yongdae's suggestion. The last thing we needed was for photographs of him turning up on Dispatch, or any of the other media outlets. We walked back in silence to the parking lot where the rented minibus waited for us.

Nate took the front seat beside me, switching the radio on, flicking through the stations. I was out of Jeju City and heading to the opposite side of the island where the resort was, when I realized what he was doing: checking the news. Much as I wanted to pull over there and then, we were on an expressway. I waited until I could pull off, ignoring the confused looks from Nate. I pushed my sunglasses onto my head, got out, stormed around to his side of the minibus, and pulled the door open. Then I threw myself at him.

It wasn't just relief—it was also the fact I could tell he was still worrying. "What's wrong?" he asked me, though his arms enveloped me.

"Nothing," I assured him, my voice muffled by his chest. I looked up and grinned. "That's the point, Nate. Yongdae has taken care of it."

I slid back out of the minibus and stepped to the side, leaning against the rear door as I stared out at the luscious foliage on the side of the road. There was a constant stream of traffic behind me, but it was strangely peaceful. I closed my eyes, tilting my head up to the sun. I knew we had to get back to the resort, but I just wanted a few minutes.

I heard Nate get out, then a shadow fell on my face. I pulled my sunglasses down to the tip of my nose so I could look at him as the sun haloed around his head. "Hey," I murmured.

His hands went either side of my head, resting against the glass. "Hey yourself," he returned, as he quickly pushed my sunglasses back up, out of the way.

"We're in a parking area on the side of the expressway," I pointed out, my hands coming up to his chest to stop him.

"And everyone is too busy, behind the minibus, driving their cars, trying not to crash," he countered.

I glanced either way, checking the few vehicles that had also pulled over. Wherever their drivers were, they weren't watching us. *To hell with it.* My hands turned to fists as I grabbed Nate's shirt and tugged him to me. He didn't fight me, his mouth claiming mine, his tongue quickly seeking entrance.

I didn't resist him, tilting my head to allow him access. We kissed hungrily. I knew Nate had been worried, but it wasn't until he was kissing me like he had thought he would never see me again, that I realized how worried he'd been. His hands moved to my face, before he finally pulled away, breathing as heavily as I was. "I am so glad you're in my life," he told me, breathlessly.

"I'm not going anywhere," I promised him.

## *H3RO*

The afternoon and evening passed in a crazy blur. It was one photoshoot after another, although, being solo shoots, it was a lot of sitting around for the others. Sadly, I wasn't afforded that luxury. I spent most of the time with Inhye, planning out what little time there was left to get other things underway.

At some point mid-afternoon, Jae and the small

team of stylists and assistants arrived. With nothing for them to do, I insisted they check into the second villa we had been assigned, and spend the day doing what they wanted.

The only member of our team who didn't go was Ahn Soomi, the talented woman who had filmed the first of H3RO's comeback videos. Our plan was to get as much of the follow up single's music video filmed while we were here, taking advantage of what the island had to offer. Soomi had already done her research, showing us her concept sketches.

"I love it," I told her, as the final part of the three-part story unfolded. With a grin as big as the Cheshire Cat's, she disappeared, off to get permission to film in her dream locations.

Sunset was around seven thirty. By the time a wrap was called, because it was dark, it felt a lot later than it was. We all piled into the minibus and I drove us back to the villa with minimal conversation. Everyone was exhausted, running on a nearly eighteen-hour day already, but equally, everyone seemed in good spirits.

"You know, tired as I am, it was days like this I missed the most," Minhyuk mumbled sleepily.

Although it wasn't a sunrise photoshoot again, the following day would have us on an island, and we needed to be on the boats at the crack of dawn. Tae and Kyun disappeared to their room almost as soon as we walked back into the villa. I watched them go with a sigh, before heading for the fridge. An evening spread had been provided earlier and the guys had eaten, I had only nibbled.

I pulled out a bowl of chopped pineapple and grabbed a fork, sitting down at the breakfast bar. With my elbow propping my head up, I could barely keep my eyes open, but I was hungry enough that if I didn't eat, I would only be up in a couple of hours snacking anyway.

"Go to bed," Minhyuk instructed me, softly.

"I'm eating this, then going," I promised him.

He stared at me, a shy look appearing in his eyes. "I'm going to bed," he told me. Then, hesitantly, he leaned in and kissed me.

I gently grabbed his shirt, tugging him to me before he could back away with little more than a peck on the lips. "Goodnight, Minhyuk," I said, pulling away.

The shy smile returned. "Goodnight, Holly."

I watched as he walked away, then turned back to pineapple. I had stabbed a chunk and raised it halfway to my mouth, before I felt eyes on me. I glanced up. Congregated in the kitchen were Dante, Nate and Jun, all staring at me with expressions varying from surprise to approval. "What?" I asked, blinking innocently.

Dante snorted. "You can quit with that innocent act, because I know you're not."

I nearly choked on my pineapple.

"What?" Jun asked, whipping his head around to face Dante.

Dante smirked. "A gentleman never talks."

"Probably not," Jun agreed, "But we're talking about you, not a gentleman." Nate clipped him around the back of the head. "Traitor!" Jun said, rubbing his head. No sooner had he dropped his hand, Dante smacked him too. "What was that for?"

"I might not be a gentleman, but Holly is a lady."

Jun hung his head. "Sorry, Holly," he muttered.

I fought to keep a straight face: it was like

watching a comedy sketch. "Go to bed, Jun."

Jun's head shot up. "Will you be joining me?" he asked, eyes sparkling. Both Dante and Nate smacked him, leaving him grumbling about violent hyungs as he sulked out of the room.

Dante yawned and stretched, then sauntered over, kissing me in a way that had my toes curling. "You can't pretend to be innocent around me, Miss Holly Lee," he whispered in my ear. "Not when I still have your panties." He reached over me, took a piece of the pineapple, and popped it in his mouth.

I glowered at the back of his head as he continued sauntering down the hallway, annoyed that I didn't have a witty comeback for him. With a sigh, I finished the last two pieces of the pineapple and got up to put my bowl and fork in the dishwasher. As I closed the door and stood upright, Nate stepped in front of me.

"Thank you for today," he said, sincerely. "In the past, Atlantis never sent anyone like Yongdae, and even our manager never came."

"I couldn't imagine not going," I told him.

"I know," he nodded, with a soft smile. "Which is why I'm even more grateful." He leaned over and pressed his lips against my cheek, then left me alone in the kitchen.

## H3RO

I'd fallen asleep as soon as my head hit the pillow, and woken confused as to why my alarm was waking me up so early. I flicked the lights on, wincing in pain. Whoever thought the idol life was a glamorous one had only ever seen the end product and clearly never seen how much effort went into getting to that. I wasn't even the one doing all the hard work!

I showered and, unmotivated to dry my hair, pulled it back into a bun. From the closet I pulled out a short playsuit, deciding that was the better option than a dress on a boat.

I hammered on all the doors as I made my way to the kitchen, then sat down at the breakfast bar waiting for a coffee to brew while I checked my emails. The others filtered in, one by one, but instead of being zombies like me, they were all bouncing about with excitement.

I finished the coffee, grumbling under my breath at Jun who was doing girl group dances around the kitchen. "Minibus!" I cried in exasperation as he moved around to Twice's 'TT'.

His exuberant mood lasted until we got to the jetty. As soon as he saw the boat, he stopped—too quickly for Dante to avoid walking into him. He ignored the annoyed swipe from Dante as he turned to me. "We're going on a boat?"

I nodded. "Today's shoot is on an island. I told you guys this yesterday."

"Jeju is an island!" Jun protested. "That's what I thought you meant." He sighed, dropping his head against Minhyuk's shoulder. "This is not going to go well."

"There, there," Minhyuk muttered, sympathetically patting his head.

I shot Jun a questioning look, but it was Dante who responded. "He gets sea sick."

"Oh," I mouthed, as Inhye and our small crew arrived.

We were shown to our two boats. They weren't small boats. With a six-member group and its entourage, as well as all the photographer, his crew and all the kit needed for a photoshoot, two boats had been chartered. While Jun stayed on dry land, and the others took their seats, we started loading in the rest of the kit on between the two vessels. It wasn't until the last minute that Jun boarded, opting to stay near the side.

It was a forty-minute trip out to the resort's private island. Until then, I'd never considered why the resort would have an island. The only thing on it seemed to be a light house. It was beautiful, but so were the beaches by the resort. Then as we rounded the island, the small huts became visible.

"They're not in use yet," one of the resort's appointed crew started explaining. "We had a storm two weeks ago which knocked the main generator out, so there's no electricity. We're waiting for a part to be shipped from China. It should be here by next week. In the meantime, we're running what we need off the emergency generator."

I couldn't help but stare longingly at the little wooden huts which stood in crystal clear shallow waters. There were little wooden bridges running between, and to a main lodge, but there was plenty of space between them for some privacy. They were pretty. Not secure enough to have an idol group stay there unless all of the huts were taken by them, but they would be amazing for a private getaway for two.

I was pondering the logistics of a private getaway for six when the retching started. The water wasn't even bumpy, especially not around here. I fished a bottle of water out of an ice box and made my way over to Jun. "I hate boats," he groaned.

# 제8 장

# H3RO

*Make It Rain*

It was another day that passed in a blur. The only difference was, not long after lunch, one of the resort crew came over to tell us we would have to wrap things up early. There was a storm coming in, and although it wasn't meant to be anything too serious, they wanted to ensure our safety and have us back on the mainland before then. While I wanted to get the shoot done, I was looking forward to the prospect of an early night.

While the resort's shoot had been taking place, Inhye, Jae, and Soomi and I had been running around, trying to get things ready for one of our other projects. There had been a number of requests on the various SNS sites for H3RO to release some behind the scenes footage, along with some self cams. OK, what their fandom was really after was for H3RO to have their own show. I couldn't provide that, but what I was going to give them was a self-videoed version of one of the other album tracks.

It was hotter today, and the boats had restricted the number of crew. As such, I had spent a lot of my time running around, making sure everyone had enough water, especially considering they were also dancing around.

It was mid-afternoon when I noticed two things. The first was the drop in temperature, brought on by an increase in wind. The second was that Jun was struggling. Earlier, I had assumed he was still recovering from the sea sickness, and I'd been doing my best to make sure he rested and stayed hydrated, but it was enough for me to call time on him.

He'd already finished up on the resort's shoot; they were now doing smaller group shots with Tae, Dante and Nate. I walked over to Inhye with a frown. "I want to get Jun off this island and to the resort's doctor. He's not well."

Inhye looked concerned. "We've not finished loading up the boats. One is nearly ready. Maybe fifteen minutes? Do you think he can hold out, or shall I get them to let half of us go?"

"Excuse me," a girl interrupted us. I turned, trying not to be rude as I barely looked at her, but not wanting to have a conversation until I worked out what to do. "I work at the resort. I'd come over to bring fresh linen ready for the guests tomorrow." She pointed to a small power boat. "I can take someone back on that, if it's an emergency? It's going to be quicker than one of those as well."

I glanced back at Jun. He was leaning against a tree. I didn't think it was life and death, but the wind was picking up, which meant the sea was getting choppier. He was already unwell and I didn't want him to suffer even more on the return trip. "Yes, please," I agreed. I looked at Inhye. "Would you mind going back with him?"

Inhye nodded. "Of course. Just let me grab my things."

"Call me and let me know how he is?"

"I will," she promised.

While she gathered her things up, I walked over to Jun and crouched down beside him. He looked up at me with a slightly dazed expression. "Do you need me to do another take?" he asked, forcing himself to get upright.

I swooped in to help him. "No, I want you to head on home."

"Are we done?" he asked, surprised.

"You are," I replied, gently. "I want you to get back to the resort and in front of the doctor."

"It's just a bit of sea sickness," he protested. I might have believed him if he hadn't leaned against me for support.

"Home, Jun," I instructed him. He sucked in a breath and nodded, insisting on walking unaided back to where the boats were docked. I turned him at the last minute, pointing him towards the smaller power boat.

"That?" he said, pulling a face.

"It will be much quicker for you," I assured him. "Which means less time on a boat."

The girl reappeared, half hidden behind a pile of dirty sheets. Moving carefully around Jun, she got on the small boat, depositing the laundry behind the seats. As she did that, I helped Jun in. He very quickly slunk into the seat and closed his eyes as he took deep breaths in through his nose and out through his mouth. "Inhye will be right here," I told both him and the girl. I looked at her and tilted my head. "I'm sorry; what's your name?"

"Dani," she replied, making her way to the front of the boat.

"Thank you, Dani. I'll see you soon, Jun."

I left them, making my way back over to the boats so I could find out how long the next boat was going to be. I was just being assured that it would only be another couple of minutes when I heard the speedboat power up. I glanced up in time to see it shooting around the island.

Good. Jun would be with a doctor soon.

I bent down to pick up a case of makeup to take on the boat, trying to hurry up the process, when I stopped and looked back at where the speedboat had gone. Something didn't feel right. "Excuse me," I called over to one of the boat hands. "Which way is the resort?"

He pointed in the opposite direction.

"Then, what's that way?"

He looked in the direction I was pointing, then up at the sky, then back to me. "Shanghai."

I could feel the blood rushing to my head. "Shanghai?" I repeated. "There's nothing else out there?"

"A whole lot of Yellow Sea?" he glanced up at the sky again. "Which someone would be a fool to take on in this."

Was I mistaken? I had to be, right? There was no way anyone would think that little boat would get them to China. I glanced up at the sky, and discovered the clouds quickly rolling in.

"We're going to have a rough crossing back," the man said, seeing me look up. With that, he returned to the task he had been doing.

I *had* to be mistaken …

But something felt … off …

I turned around, about to follow the path around the huts, down to the beach which curved around in that direction, when I saw Inhye. I ran over to her. "What are you doing here?"

"What are you doing here?" she asked me.

"Boat's ready!" someone yelled. "Those getting on, get on!"

"The girl said you'd told her to tell me that you'd changed your mind. You'd gone to grab your phone, and you were going to go back with Jun."

"I told her to wait for you," I said. I took a deep breath. "OK, there has to be a logical explanation for this. Maybe Jun felt worse and she thought she needed to go."

"That makes sense," Inhye nodded, pulling out her phone. "She won't have made it back to the island yet, but I can make sure someone from the resort is there to meet them with the resort's medical staff," she said, walking away to make the call.

As she moved away, Dante, Nate, and Minhyuk joined me, Tae and Kyun lingering nearby. "Is everything OK?" Minhyuk asked.

I gave him a bright smile as I nodded my head. "Yes. You guys go get on the boat and get back to the villa. We're calling it a wrap early because of the incoming storm, so we get the evening to ourselves."

"Yes!" Nate and Dante exclaimed, giving each other high fives, before hurrying onto the boat.

"Where's Jun?" Minhyuk asked.

"I sent him back already," I told him, truthfully.

"He wasn't feeling well and I was hoping to get him back before the water got too rough and unbearable for him." I looked out to see and frowned. "I have a feeling our trip back will be far from the smooth crossing it was this morning."

Minhyuk didn't take his eyes off me. "Is Jun OK?"

I sighed. "Honestly, I think he's been out in the sun too long. He started the day throwing up, and it has been very hot today. You've all been working hard and I think he's dehydrated. I'm sure that the doctor will see him and say the same thing. So, let's get back, pick him up, and let him get a good night's sleep."

I didn't lie to Minhyuk. Even though I wasn't a doctor, I didn't think his condition was too serious. However, the nagging feeling in the back of my head was telling me that Jun wasn't on the way back to the resort. Minhyuk, however, despite looking concerned for his younger groupmate, nodded and boarded the boat.

I turned to Tae and Kyun. They were both watching me, betrayal still shining in their eyes. I waved them on the boat, then glanced back at the end of the island Jun had disappeared to.

"I spoke to the manager," Inhye declared, rejoining my side. "The reception is dropping out because of this storm, but he said he would have people waiting for them at the jetty, and not to worry."

"That's good to know," I agreed.

"But?" she asked.

"Nothing," I said with a smile and a shake of my head. "You get back with the others," I added as the captain yelled out a last call for that boat. "I'll get the next one with Jae."

"What about you?"

"I need to check something," I said. I knew I had to be wrong, but I couldn't shake the feeling that something wasn't right. The only way that was going to happen was to see it with my own eyes. I didn't pay any attention to what she was saying to me as I walked away.

"Next boat will be twenty minutes!" she yelled after me.

"I only need five," I called before I disappeared behind a hut. "I hope I only need five," I muttered to myself, picking up my pace.

As the wooden boardwalk descended to the beach, the rain started to fall. It wasn't hard, but it was enough to make me wish I'd thought to bring an umbrella or jacket with me. Oh well …

I made it to the 'corner', only it wasn't quite the corner. It was a misleading corner and with the tide coming in, I was going to have to leap between rock pools to get where I needed to. I had just jumped to a rock when a voice called out, startling me. "Where are you going?"

I only just kept my balance. "Kyun, why aren't you on that boat?" I demanded.

"Why aren't you?" he asked.

"I needed to check something out before we left," I told him. "Go back to the boat before it leaves."

"It already left," Kyun shrugged.

"Then go back and wait for the second one."

Kyun folded his arms. "Why are you out here?"

I rolled my eyes and let out an exasperated sigh. "Because I need to make sure I'm not seeing things."

"What things?"

"Jun. OK? I sent Jun back on a boat because he wasn't feeling well, only I could have sworn that he went this way, and apparently the only place you'll get to if you head this way is China, I just want to make sure I'm not hallucinating. OK?"

Kyun shook his head. "Holly, that's crazy. The only thing you'll find if you go this way is yourself getting hurt. Come back to the—"

"Help!"

I froze. The word was faint, and I could have imagined it over the growing waves crashing against the rocks. A particularly large one hit the rock next to me then. I went flying backwards into the rockpool, only just missing hitting my head on the volcanic stone the island was made from.

The next thing I knew, Kyun was in the water with me, helping me up as another wave crashed over us. "Come on," he said, tugging me back to the resort's huts.

"Help!"

Kyun looked at me, his eyes growing wide. "You heard that too, right?" I asked him. He nodded. I scrambled out of the rock pool, fighting against the rising water to get through the cove to the other side. Kyun was right beside me, helping me through the water which seemed less like a tropical ocean and more like Lake Michigan.

By the time we made it to the far side, the beach was almost gone. The rain was lashing down on us and the wind was so icy that I was shivering.

"Help!" the voice yelled again.

"That's Jun!" Kyun cried.

We charged along the beach, finally rounding the

corner. I spotted him instantly. He was trying, and struggling, to pull something up what little of the beach there was. We ran over. It was the girl who was supposed to be taking them back to the resort. Kyun grabbed under one of her armpits, while Jun moved over to the other, pulling her up, out of the water.

They laid her on the ground, and I dropped to my knees beside her. She wasn't breathing. "Go back and get help," I instructed them knowing she needed CPR. I sent a silent prayer I could remember how to do it correctly. Kyun took off back the way we had come from, while Jun sank to the sand beside us.

He was still upright and breathing, even though he had gone gray, so I ignored him. Instead, I tilted the girl's head back and gave her two deep breaths before trying to remember where it was I needed to do chest compressions. Hoping I was right, I started pumping, physically wincing when I felt her ribs crack beneath me.

If it wasn't for the person who had trained me saying that frequently happened, I would have freaked out. I kept on going, then gave her two more breaths. I was midway through the next round of compressions, already feeling exhausted, when she coughed up water. "Jun, help me," I said, trying to roll her on her side. Jun reached over and pulled with me, and she finished coughing.

"She's not waking up," Jun said, his eyes wide with fear.

I shook my head. "She's breathing," I said, hoping that was enough. "She's going to need a doctor." I relaxed back on to my knees, just as thunder and lightning cracked across the sky. I jumped, unprepared for the noise rather than being scared of the weather.

"We just need to get out of here."

I knew that was not going to happen when I looked up and saw Kyun running back to us, alone.

# 제9 장

# H3R오

*Might Just Die*

"The sea is too rough to get back over the rocks," Kyun said, joining us.

"OK," I muttered more to myself. "We're not getting back to the mainland tonight," I said aloud. "The boats have gone and it will be nearly an hour before they realize we weren't on either of them." I turned to Jun. He was still hanging on, but I could tell he was struggling. "Do you think you can walk if I help you?"

He nodded. "I'm fine."

I doubted that, but I wasn't going to argue. "Kyun, do you think you can manage to carry her?" I asked, pointing at the unconscious girl.

"Yes," he said.

"We might luck out and they might send another boat out tonight, but let's assume the worst and that we're going to be here overnight."

"What are you thinking?" Jun asked, weakly.

"We cut through that," I pointed at the foliage behind us. "Head back to those huts and stay in one of them."

"That sounds like a good idea," Kyun agreed. He crouched down beside the girl and I helped him get her on his back. He started walking towards the trees. I got up, offering my hand to Jun, who took it. I helped him up, but he didn't let go.

It was easier to walk through the forest than on the beach. The ground, though slippery, was firmer, and the rain wasn't lashing in our faces. It was probably as slow going as getting across the rocks had been, but it was much safer.

It was also eerily quiet. I tried to quieten my brain which was going into overdrive at all the things that could be lurking in the bushes … snakes … wild boars … monsters … axe murderers … I'd watched too many horror shows.

Thankfully, the overgrowth eventually began to thin out, opening up to what was left of the beach by the huts. The tide had come in and the first half of the bridge up to the walkway was under water, but we pushed through. Kyun headed straight for the first hut, but I stopped him. "Go for the one we were using today. If nothing else, I know Dani brought clean linen over."

"Who's Dani?" Kyun asked, changing direction.

"The girl on your back," I told him as we reached the door.

Thankfully it was unlocked and we bustled in. The wind and rain fought against us shutting the door, but we managed to shut the cold and wet out. I stood there, trying to catch my breath as I looked around the hut. I hadn't had a chance to explore one earlier.

It was like an open-planned mini apartment with large chunks of the floor being made of glass to see the water below. There was a small kitchen with a breakfast bar in one corner, opening out to couches that looked like clouds facing a large window which opened up to a private outside area. In the sun, it would have been a view of a tropical paradise, but all I could see in the dimming light was rain pounding against the glass.

At the back, behind a privacy screen, was an enormous bed, leading off to a bathroom. It was the perfect location for a honeymoon. Tonight, it was also a perfect location for shelter.

A pile of linen lay on the unmade bed. I kicked my sandals off, cringing at the coldness of the glass floor beneath me, and hurried over to the carpeted area surrounding the bed, showering dirty water everywhere. "Kyun, put her down on the couch. I'm going to get her out of those wet clothes and wrap her in these to warm her up." As Kyun laid her down, I turned to Jun. "You two go in the bathroom. If the hot water is working, take a shower. If it's not, like I suspect, get out of your clothes and wrap up in a couple of these blankets."

Jun nodded and walked to the bathroom, taking some sheets with him. I joined Kyun by the couch, wondering what was taking him so long. "Are you OK?" I asked him.

He pointed at the girl. "Does she look familiar to you?"

I peered down and shrugged. There had been a lot of people on the sets over the last two days. "Not really," I said, suddenly feeling bad about that. I had gone to Lee Woojin recently and he had impressed me by knowing the names of everyone we had met. I was certain he knew the names of everybody at Atlantis. Sure, she was the resort staff, but I was willing to bet that if Woojin was here, he would have known her name.

"Isn't she the girl who was all over Nate in those photographs?" he asked.

I tilted my head to see her face better. The sea water had turned her into a panda and with half of her hair having escaped from its ponytail and now plastered to her face, I wasn't sure. "I mean, it looks like her," I agreed, frowning. "But why would she be here? Why would she be trying to sail off to China with Jun?"

"Who is trying to sail to China with me?" Jun asked, appearing beside us wrapped up in several blankets. He didn't look completely better, but a bit of color had returned to his face.

I held my hands up. "This conversation can wait. Kyun, go get out of your wet clothes. Jun, go with him so I can help her." I waited for them to both disappear into the bathroom, then made short work of the girl's clothes. I wrapped her up in the blankets as best I could. She was still unconscious, and it left me a little worried, but I was not a doctor and there was nothing else I could think of doing that would help her, aside from getting her to a hospital.

Once I was certain she was bundled up in a tight cocoon, I turned my attention to myself. I was only wearing the thin jumpsuit, but I was shivering so much, I was surprised I'd managed to get Dani's clothes off her. I quickly stripped down to my underwear, then dried myself off with a towel before wrapping a couple of blankets around me.

"You guys can come out now," I called as I moved across to the bed. There were a couple of sheets left and I opened them out over the bed so they could crawl under them.

Jun walked out with the blankets still over his head. "The water is working, but it's cold," he said.

"That doesn't surprise me," I shrugged, pointing at the bed. "In. You need to rest."

Jun nodded and climbed in without protest. I looked to Kyun, but he avoided my eyes and walked past me into the main area. This was going to be a long night.

Figuring we didn't have much time left before the light disappeared completely, I decided to explore the little hut. The wardrobe in the bedroom had a small pile of disposable slippers and I pulled them out, taking a pair for myself. It also had a box of toiletries— shampoo, conditioner and soap—none of which was particularly helpful.

However, finding the box of individually wrapped chocolates was like hitting the jackpot. I was exhausted and hungry. They weren't nutritional, but there would be a nice sugar rush for the energy boost. I pulled the box out and took them over to the bed. As soon as Jun saw them, his eyes lit up and he grabbed a handful. "Just eat them slowly," I warned him. "We don't need you throwing up again." I moved over to the kitchen area and found Kyun with his head in one of the cupboards. "Anything useful?" I asked.

"Candles and matches," he replied, shortly.

Leaving him to deal with that, I moved back to the couches, unable to stop myself from checking on Dani. She was still OK. I scooped up the clothes and took them to the bathroom, wringing them—and the guy's things—out so I could hang them up to hopefully dry.

I returned to the living room to retrieve my phone. I had taken it out of my pocket before I had taken my clothes off. I hadn't dared to try it before, certain it was dead. I pressed the home button … nothing. "Figures," I muttered, tossing it back down on the table. It had been fully submerged in the sea before the rain had continued the job of soaking it.

I stared out the window. The storm showed no sign of letting up as the thunder and lightning continued above us. The huts were very sturdy—even with the waves lashing up against them, they barely swayed. Outside was a no-go, though. The waves were sweeping over the walkways. I shuddered, bringing the blankets closer around me.

With one last look at the turbulent weather, I turned and walked over to the kitchen. Kyun had left, having gone to the bedroom to light the candles. I pulled a jug out of the cupboard and filled it with water. It was clear and cold, and tasted fresh, thankfully. Making sure to grab some glasses, I shuffled back to the bedroom to join the other two.

After making sure Jun had drunk a full glass, I crawled up onto the foot of the bed and sat, crossing my legs beneath me. After helping myself to a handful of chocolate, I turned to Jun. "What happened?"

"I don't really remember," he admitted. "I was pretty out of it when I got in the boat. I know we'd barely gotten out of here when a massive wave hit us and capsized us. I grabbed her and pulled us both to shore. Who is she?"

"I'm sorry," I apologized, hanging my head. "I thought she was a resort employee. She said she could get you back to the mainland and the resort's doctors quickly. I should have known."

"How could you have known?" Jun asked with a frown. "She was wearing the resort's uniform."

"Jun's right," Kyun said, quietly. "If anything, it's the resort with a security issue."

"I should have checked her ID," I shrugged. "I should have recognized her."

"How could you have recognized her?" Jun cried in surprise.

"Kyun thinks she's the girl who was all over Nate in the club; the one who spiked his drink."

Jun leaned to the side, peering around the room divider to the girl on the couch. "I can't tell from here." He leaned back with a frown. "But even if she is, why did you think she was taking me to China?"

"You didn't go in the direction of the resort. One of the boat captains said the only thing in the direction you went was China," I explained.

"But this doesn't make any sense," Jun disagreed. "If you ignore the fact that little boat was never going to make it across the ocean, why would she take me? Isn't she Nate's sasaeng?"

"Maybe she likes you all?" I suggested with a shrug. I couldn't fault her for *that*. Her execution, however …

"Then should we tie her up?" Kyun asked.

I glanced back at her and shook my head. "She isn't going anywhere in weather like this."

"I meant for our protection!"

"With what?" I asked him. "She's unconscious and there's nothing in here to tie her up with."

"Even so, she managed to sail off with Jun," Kyun reminded me. As if I could forget that.

I chewed at my lip. He was right, but unless I started ripping up sheets, there was nothing useable. Plus, there was something about tying up an unconscious girl which seemed wrong.

"I think we'll be fine," Jun said with a yawn. "And either way, my head hurts too much to care right now. I'm going to sleep." He settled down onto the mattress and closed his eyes. Minutes later, he was asleep.

"I wish I had that skill," I muttered. I glanced over at Kyun who was purposely not looking at me. This was going to be a long night. My body was exhausted, but I was too anxious to sleep. It made no sense that anyone would come back here with the weather like this, but I couldn't help but feel that if I did fall asleep, they would return and we would miss them.

I got up and wandered over to the couches. If I was going to stay awake, I was going to put it to good use and keep an eye on the crazy girl. I alternated my attention between her and out the window. There was very little to see outside. Night time had set in and the little light from the candles wasn't enough to illuminate outside. It felt like the storm was easing off though.

These huts were no longer feeling all that romantic.

Part way through the storm—I wasn't sure if hours had passed or minutes—I went back to check on Jun and Kyun. Both were fast asleep. I had been expecting to find Kyun awake still, but seeing as he was next to Jun, I guess he found the comfort he needed.

I blew out the candles before I made my way back to my spot on the second couch. The wind finally seemed to be dying down as the waves didn't look as big anymore.

At some point, I nodded off. When I awoke, the room was brighter. I peered blurry eyed out of the window. The water was still choppy, but the rain was finally a steady patter against the glass.

It was then that I realized that the hairs on the back of my neck were on end. I glanced around the room, trying to work out what was bothering me, but couldn't see anything. I settled back down figuring it was the unease of being stuck on this island, when I heard a strange sound. With no electricity, the room was eerily quiet, apart from the sound of soft snores.

And a kind of slurping sound.

I frowned, my gaze falling on the empty couch next to me …

Then I was on my feet, charging across the room. Dani was straddling Jun, bent over, kissing his face. Jun, the person who could sleep through anything, grunted, brought the blankets tighter to him, and carried on sleeping.

"Oh, hell no!" I yelled, leaping over. Kyun's eyes shot open, but before he could react, my hands wrapped around the girl's ponytail, yanking her backwards and off Jun—and the bed.

She screamed as she fell to the floor, but before she could get back up, I kicked her over with the back of my foot, and dropped down on her, firmly, with my knee in the center of her back. When she reached up to claw at me, I grabbed her wrist, twisting it up behind her back.

"What the hell?" Jun asked. He was upright beside Kyun, the pair of them staring in confused horror at the pair of us.

"That's exactly what I want to know," I

demanded.

"Get off me!" she screeched.

There was a flash of light, and then the door to the hut burst open.

# 제10 장

# H3RO

*Bad Mama Jama*

"Thank you, Miss Lee," the police officer said, closing his book. It was the same officer who I had spoken to with Yongdae, which had made things slightly easier. I also had Yongdae with me, even though he really wasn't needed, but the company was appreciated. That being said, it had been a very long couple of hours in that room.

The rescue party—resort employees, not the coast guard—had returned to the island as soon as the storm had passed, arriving almost on time to save the day. After some initial confusion, they had taken Dani onto the boat and into 'custody'.

The crew had helped Kyun, Jun, and myself onto the boat and taken us back to the resort. Unfortunately for Jun, the return trip had been just as miserable as his trip out there.

As soon as we'd made it to land, we'd been whisked away in the back of an ambulance to the hospital. I'd considered protesting seeing as my injuries were scrapes and bruises from where the waves had knocked me into the rocks, but going meant I stayed with Kyun and Jun.

Kyun and I got discharged quickly. The doctors wanted Jun to stay in for a few more hours, just to give him some more fluids. That was when the rest of H3RO arrived with Inhye, carrying in several bags of nutritional McDonalds meals. While the doctor turned a blind eye, the eight of us tucked in. I was famished.

We all left together and when we got to the villa, Yongdae was already waiting for us. Inhye had made the call as soon as she had seen Dani being loaded into the back of a police car and Yongdae had taken the next flight out of Incheon. An officer had told her we would be required to make statements as soon as possible. Insisting we get it done straight away so charges could be made, Yongdae had taken the three of us to the police station.

"There is a car waiting to take you back to the resort," Yongdae told me before we finally left the station. "There are a few reporters outside already," he added. "Keep your heads down, move straight to the car, and do not answer any questions. I will make a statement, then return to Seoul to follow up with Atlantis there."

"Thank you for coming all this way again," I told him, sincerely grateful. He gave me a nod, then indicated to the door. Yongdae did as he said, talking to the reporters while we hurried into the car. We didn't escape attention completely, but the crowd was small enough that we left the station without too much trouble. I had a feeling that if this was Seoul, that would have been a different story.

At some point on the way back to the resort, I fell asleep, only waking when the driver was gently prodding me. I did the same for Kyun and Jun who, in the back of the car, had fallen asleep against each other.

The villa was empty. I had insisted that the others continue with the schedule as best they could, leaving it to Inhye to explain to the resort why they were two members down. I didn't expect the resort to complain—it was the least they could do considering someone had breached their security. I also wanted the others to carry on and not worry about us.

An email had arrived from Inhye while we'd been in the station. We were free for the day. While other individual shots for the sportswear were taking place tomorrow, Kyun and Jun would be able to get theirs completed with the shots for their suits which the others were completing today.

"The good news is that we have the rest of the day off," I said as we walked into the villa. I yawned and stretched. "I don't know about you guys, but I am going to shower and nap."

"Sounds like a good idea," Jun mumbled. He leaned over and kissed me, then walked off towards his room like a zombie. I watched him go, wincing slightly: Kyun had witnessed the whole thing. I was certain that Jun's kiss had been almost automatic, given how tired he was. I didn't think he'd done it with the intention of upsetting Kyun, especially as he knew how he felt about everything.

But Kyun's face had taken on a frown and he walked off without saying anything.

I rubbed my face with my hands, then blew out a breath. In the end, I went up to my room and into the bathroom. Inhye had brought clothes to the hospital for us to change into, but I'd never had the opportunity to shower before dressing and going to the police station.

My hair was still in a bun, though loose tendrils were hanging haphazardly everywhere. It had moved from beach-hair-chic into walked-through-a-hedge-backwards. Thanks to the drenching in sea water, it was also quite crispy. I snapped the band to free the hair and it barely moved; the saltwater acting like a strong hairspray. There was no way I was running a brush through it until I had soaked it in conditioner.

Like my hair, my skin had a sea salt coating, leaving me feeling dry and itchy. My legs, which had been hidden under a pair of trousers, were also covered in dried mud. The shower was practically calling out to me.

The shower was four times as big as the one back at the dorm. Instead of a shower curtain, there was glass with strategically placed frosted sections. I turned the water on. It came out hot almost instantly. I just stood there, my eyes closed, trying to find the energy to get in so I could start washing my hair. Now that the adrenaline of everything was wearing off, I was exhausted.

There was a knock at the door, and I sighed, reaching for a robe before wrapping it around my body. "Hello?" I called, expecting it to be Jun.

Kyun's head appeared around the door, but he kept his eyes on the floor. "Can we talk?"

I gave the shower a longing look before I turned it off. Much as I wanted it, there was something about Kyun's tone that told me this conversation had to be had now. I followed him out into the bedroom watching as he paced back and forth a few times.

With an inward sigh, I moved towards the

balcony doors and opened them, gesturing that Kyun should follow. I took a seat on one of the chairs, staring out across the ocean view as I waited for Kyun to join me. The sun was high in the sky, and the temperature back to hot and humid. The only reminder of the previous day's storm seemed to be the dirt on my legs.

Kyun stepped outside, taking the other seat. He was still in the clothes Inhye had brought for him to the hospital. Although I'd not paid much attention before, the salt water had made his hair stick out in all kinds of angles, but unlike mine, it looked cute.

"I can't sleep," he admitted.

I nodded in understanding. I hadn't thought about that when I'd sent him off to bed. The reason he shared a bed with Tae was because something had happened to him in his past and he couldn't sleep alone. I was no longer surprised at how uncomfortable he looked, though I was curious as to why he hadn't gone to Jun.

"Kyun, nothing has changed on my part," I told him, gently. "You are always welcome to sleep with me."

"No," he quickly said, then sighed. "No, that's not what I mean."

"OK?" I said, now confused.

"I thought you were going to die," he blurted out.

My eyes widened: that was the last thing I expected him to say. "Under normal circumstances, I probably would have panicked, because I'm really not a fighter, but I think the adrenaline—"

"I don't mean you taking on that sasaeng," he said with a shake of his head. He got up and walked over to the edge of the balcony, resting his forearms on the metal railing.

When he didn't continue, I got up and joined his side, keeping a respectful distance. "Then when?" I asked, gently.

"When that wave hit you."

"It wasn't that big," I said. "Plus, there was a giant pool of water."

Kyun turned to glower at me. "That wave was taller than you, and it knocked you backwards into a *rock* pool. You could have hit your head. You could have gone the other way and been pulled out to sea." The glower darkened. "Damnit, Holly, we could have lost you."

"And if I hadn't, we would have lost Jun," I snapped back. "He would have been left alone on that island with that crazy ass woman and who knows what would have happened."

"She would have been dead," he retorted. "We pulled her out of the water and *you* revived her!"

"Don't you dare yell at me for saving someone's life," I cried, furious at his words. "I don't care who she is."

Kyun closed his eyes, then turned his head away with a slight shake of his head. "That's not ..." Then he turned fully to face me. "Holly, I love you, OK? The fact that I nearly lost you ..." he shook his head again. "Don't do stupid shit that puts your life in danger because losing you would be like losing one of H3RO, and I would not survive that."

I blinked a few times, too stunned to respond as I processed his words. Unfortunately, that was the wrong response. Looking both upset and embarrassed, Kyun turned away. "I knew it was too late, I'm sorry," he muttered, starting to walk back into the bedroom to make his escaped.

Without thinking, I reached after him and grabbed his hand. "Wait!" I cried. He stopped, but didn't turn around. "Kyun, you surprised me," I admitted.

The hand I was holding gripped back. Slowly, Kyun turned to face me. "It's not too late?"

I shook my head.

Kyun stepped towards me, taking my other hand, and then our toes were touching. I felt like I'd stumbled across a rare wild animal and if I moved I would send it running for cover, so I stood perfectly still. His eyes were fixed on mine, then they dropped to my lips. I thought he was going to kiss me then, but he didn't, instead wetting his.

I held my breath, wondering where this uncertain Kyun had come from. His last kiss had been like he was claiming me as his own. It had come out of nowhere and had been rough and firm. This was like a whole new Kyun in front of me. He swallowed and licked his lips again. He was nervous.

I was about to help him out, taking the lead to show him this was OK, but he moved.

Slowly.

I could feel my heartbeat quicken, unlike his movements which seemed to slow even more as he brought his mouth towards mine. Finally, his lips made contact with mine. The kiss seemed almost shy at first, like he was testing the waters … maybe he thought *I* was a wild animal he could startle easily too?

Slowly, one of his hands left mine, tracing my arm upwards, before gently settling on my face. His other hand wrapped around my back, pulling me closer to him with a gentle tug. I complied, bringing my hands around his back. Like my touch was a signal he was waiting for, he urged my lips open with his tongue.

And then I stopped things, pulling away.

The moment I did, Kyun let go, taking two steps away from me as rejection appeared in his eyes.

"I want to continue this, I really do," I promised him. "But things are still as they were, Kyun," I explained, as gently as possible. "I love you. I love you so much that these last few days have hurt me not being able to spend time in the same room as you, but I love the others too. I know I am asking too much of all of you, and I know that you're not happy or comfortable with that, but I don't want this to make you think that I'm choosing you over the others." A lump appeared in my throat, and I pushed it down. "I can't do that."

"I know," Kyun said, simply.

# 제11 장

# *H3RO*

*You In Me*

"I meant what I said before," he said. "I couldn't survive losing you or H3RO. I might be in love with you, but I love H3RO too. It might be selfish, but I realized I could have it all." He chewed his lip, thoughtfully. "I thought it was a crazy idea, and the fact it came from Jun didn't really sell it, but now that I've given it some more thought, I don't think it's that crazy at all. Different, yes, and I'm still not completely sure how it will work, but it's not a bad idea at all. I love you, and I love them too."

"Do you really mean that?" I asked.

Kyun nodded. "Yes." As if to prove it, he was back in front of me before I could blink, his arms wrapping around me to pull me flush against him. Then he titled his head, closing the distance between us. His kiss was soft and warm, somewhere in the middle of our rough first kiss, and the last hesitant kiss, but like with both, it left me feeling breathless.

"You were about to take a shower," he murmured.

I grinned. "Want to join me?"

His response was physical, tugging me back into my room and towards the bathroom. We wasted no time in getting naked and in the shower, but it wasn't until we were under the hot water that Kyun paused again. He stepped back, out of the water and stared at me with a look that sent anticipation radiating through me.

Then, he surprised me by turning me around. Before I could question anything, he was leaning up against me, his mouth against my neck, sucking at a spot that had my hand shooting against the wall to steady myself. I closed my eyes and moaned; a sound, I discovered, excited him as his teeth gently nipped at me.

An arm wrapped around my waist, keeping me firmly locked against him as he took a step back, bringing me with him so the water was on my chest and off my face.

Then his hands were on me, only, they were on my head. The scent of shampoo assaulted my nostrils as his fingers worked my hair instead of other areas of my body I wanted them. "Kyun," I groaned.

He leaned forward and nipped at my neck. "Be patient," he chided me, before urging me back under the water.

I could feel his arousal against the small of my back, which was not helping matters. How the hell he could stand there so calmly I don't know, because I was getting increasingly frustrated.

To speed up the process, I took some shampoo and then turned. *Holy hell*, that was a mistake, because now that arousal was pressed up somewhere else. In front of me, Kyun opened his mouth, but before he could say anything, I was shampooing his hair for him.

He gritted his teeth, but said nothing. Then a mischievous grin appeared.

The next thing I knew, he was crouched down in front of me. My body was protecting him from most of the water spray. His hands went for … my feet. The confusion took a moment to clear until he slowly lifted one in the air, so I could put my hands out for balance. He soaped them clean, one at a time. His hands and soap worked up my left leg. Just as he reached the top, he paused, and looked up at me.

I clamped my teeth down on my lip as his head hovered in front of me. Then, before I could work my fingers through his hair, he had dropped down to my right ankle. I let out a low growl from the back of my throat before I could stop myself, which set Kyun chuckling.

I hadn't heard that before. I liked it.

Once again, his hands set off on a painstakingly drawn-out trip up my leg. Once again, he stopped right by the top. I sucked a breath in …

And he stood up.

I tilted my head at him, but he merely smiled and started washing my arms, ignoring the fact that I was all hot and flustered and it wasn't caused by the temperature of the water.

After gently cleaning my back, finally, I snapped, turning to him and sticking my chest out at him. "Do you expect me to clean these myself?"

"Not likely," Kyun muttered, and he then proceeded to *wash* them.

I was so worked up, I was ready to turn the water cold.

As his fingers moved south to my intimate area, I

grew excited again, but once again, I was left disappointed. Kyun's eyes caught mine, and he smirked.

I was about to take matters into my own hands when he started cleaning himself. "Oh, to hell with this," I grumbled, taking the soap from him. It was high time he caught some of his own medicine. I slowly dropped down, though not before using his body as a pole, rubbing up against him. I smiled to myself when he let out a hiss. I didn't have the patience to work up his legs as slowly as he had mine, but I did take my time with his chest, especially when cleaning his small H3RO tattoo. Sitting over his heart, they were as precious to him as they were to me.

I leaned forward to his ear as my hands worked over his shoulders. "You're not the only one who can be a tease."

Kyun narrowed his eyes, then brought his hands up to my head, pulling it over so he could kiss me. As his tongue worked open my mouth and started moving against mine, in a very deliberate movement, he pushed his groin against me.

I forced my hand between us, heading straight for his erection. He groaned into my mouth as my hand wrapped around him. One hand left my head, and the judder told me it was against the wall. Then, I was moved out of the water. I could tell what he was trying to do, but instead of letting go, I worked my hand up and down his thick shaft.

At that moment, my back was pushed up against the icy tiles of the wall. I gasped in shock, at both the cold against my skin, and as the action had my sensitive nipples rubbing against his chest. Although it had me stop kissing him, I refused to let go of him, instead making the motion more of a turn.

Apparently, that was the right thing to do. Kyun's head fell forward towards my collarbone, and he bit down on the sensitive area muffling his groan. He was close, I could tell.

Then, he stepped back separating the two of us, and turned off the water. He reached for a towel, using it to rub at my hair. "Really?" I asked, from under it. "Do you know how frustrating you are?"

"I think you're the one who is frustrated," Kyun disagreed.

He wasn't wrong, but before I could tell him that, his tongue was distracting mine once more. He threw the towel to one side as I wrapped my arms around his neck.

He scooped me up, his mouth never leaving mine, but his kiss remained steady, despite my best efforts. He carried me into the bedroom, lying me down on the bed, then he stood up. Kyun stared down at me, his eyes scanning over my body once more.

*Holy hell*, this guy was going to kill me. Before he could stop me, I had moved to the side of my bed where my purse was hiding. I reached in, pulled out a condom, then tossed it to him. "For the love of god, will you put that on and fuck me already?"

Kyun reached over, but instead of picking up the foil packet, wrapped his hands around my ankles and tugged me back down the bed towards him. "That's what I did last time."

I grunted in frustration. "Well, if you want to watch, you're more than welcome to." I started moving my hands and he was suddenly on the bed, straddling me. His thighs were either side of mine, pressing them closed, while his hands grabbed my wrists, holding them down by the side of my head.

"Don't you dare," he threatened me, his face close to mine. I could feel his erection, pressed up between us.

"How is this not killing you?" I asked, my words somewhere between a moan and a whine.

His mouth moved to my neck and he slowly kissed and sucked at it, following the curve of my collarbone. "Because I know what's coming," Kyun murmured.

That promise sent a shiver down my spine.

He shifted his weight, and then his knee was prizing my legs apart. When I spread them, eager, he set his knee back down, just inches too low for me to be able to work out some of my frustrations. "Oh, come on!" I objected.

Kyun pulled back and looked down at me. Water dripped off from his hair onto my cheek, but I was more distracted by the arctic breeze from the air conditioning whipping across my nipples. "Holly, will you shut up?" There was no real question to his demand. "The only thing I want to hear from your mouth is you shouting my name."

I swear I almost orgasmed right there.

Kyun brought his mouth back to mine and continued with the long and slow movements of his tongue. Finally, he moved on to a new form of torture. He let go of my hands, and while never breaking the kiss, maneuvered them underneath me. When I arched my back up, he used one hand to push me back down and hold me there. He might not have had a set of abs like Dante or Nate, but he damn well had some core strength.

By the time his mouth started trailing kisses back down my neck and latched on to one of my nipples, I was squirming beneath him and I couldn't even tell the air conditioning was on anymore.

Finally … *finally*, his hand moved south. I was so sensitive, that it didn't take more than a few fingers moving in and out of me, working at me, for me to be granting Kyun's wish and have me yelling his name.

In a haze of pleasure, I barely realized when he sat back, and I had no clue, no curiosity as to what was going on. He waited until I was almost coherent again, and then I felt him enter me. He took his time, waiting for me to adjust to his width, easing in inch by inch.

Pausing, he resumed his kisses, then with the same deliberate pace, he started moving in and out of me, ignoring my efforts to hurry the torture up. I had never realized Kyun was such a tormentor.

His pace began to quicken, his thrusts becoming deeper and more urgent. The change did exactly what I needed it to, and once again, I was yelling his name. Kyun continued in his movements until I felt him join me.

He collapsed on top of me, breathing as heavily as I was. I wrapped my arms around him, feeling reassurance in his weight. Finally, he slid off me, disappearing into the bathroom. I lay there, staring up at the ceiling not moving until he came out and settled down beside me.

I rolled onto my side, moving my arm under my ear. "Are you really OK with everything?" I asked him.

He shrugged. "I'm not going to deny that I'm not always going to find this easy, but I meant it, Holly. I love you, and I love them. We might not have a future with H3RO, but I feel certain we have a future together, whatever that future is."

I reached out, running my finger over his tattoo as I gave him a soft smile. That was something else that had been lingering in the back of my mind. I hadn't wanted to mention it because of everything else that was going on, but we still owed Atlantis another number one single.

Our promotions for 'Who is Your Hero?' would have ended this week if it wasn't for this trip to Jeju. Although we'd pushed back all of them, the truth was, with a ten-day break, we might as well not continue. New songs had been released, and the song had dropped off the charts. We were only insisting on them happening still because we didn't want to disappoint the fans.

I got off the bed, he frowned. "Where are you going?"

"For a shower."

"Want some company?" he asked, wiggling his eyebrows at me.

I looked back at him and cocked my head. "Not a chance," I told him, leaving him chuckling to himself on the bed.

# 제12 장

# *H3RO*

*Twins (Knock Out)*

O ur last full day on Jeju Island rolled around quickly. It coincided with what would have been the last day of promotions and under normal circumstances, this comeback would have exhausted any idol. Given how much H3RO had been through, I was impressed they were still standing. As it was, they still had one last week of the postponed schedule before we were officially finished. They also had to get today's shoot wrapped up before the birthday party they were performing at tonight.

It was another early morning wakeup call. This time, we could stay in the villa while hair and makeup was done. Kyun was up first—Jae needed to reapply the silver hair dye as it had almost disappeared.

Soomi and her crew were already at the first site, setting up. She'd gotten permission to film at two of them. Thankfully, Jeju Island wasn't that big and it wouldn't take us too long to get between the two locations.

Last night, Soomi had spent a couple of hours at the villa going over her vision with them. I'd been contemplating asking them if they wanted to spend the day resting, but once I'd told them that we were going to make use of the scenery while we were here, there was no comeback imminent and they would have some time off before we dived into the madness again, they had all seemed eager.

The only one who had seemed concerned was Tae, and that was because of the cast on his arm. "It's one thing to hide it in a photoshoot, but in a music video? It will be gone by the time we film the rest of it."

"Actually, it's perfect for the story," Soomi had told him, before launching into an excited babble about how she was going have someone injured.

"Besides," I added. "We're only doing the story part here. With the cuts to the dance scenes, you'll have different hair and styling anyway, so it won't matter."

Jae and his two-woman team were quick and efficient and we were in the minibus ahead of schedule. They'd also showed off just how talented they were.

For most of this video storyline, H3RO were going to be held captive. They'd been given a similar set of clothing to what they'd been in for the previous part of the story, only these clothes were more tattered. I was not complaining at all the rips and tears which gave me sneaky glimpses of arms, thighs and abs. The makeup was also made to look like they were a little beaten. The team were coming with us to apply more makeup as the story unfolded.

They'd managed to make all six members look convincingly hurt and injured, while still making them look as hot as sin. Every time I found myself looking up into the rearview mirror and stealing glances at them, I had to remind myself they didn't need tending to.

We arrived at the first location before sunrise. Soomi and her crew had set up the lights and props and the abandoned school was now looking like a prison or a dungeon. "Is there something you want to tell me?" I asked Soomi as we set up for the first take—one that had H3RO chained up. It wasn't until the younger woman looked majorly embarrassed at my question and all but ran away, that I remembered this was not Kate I was talking to.

Which reminded me … feeling mischievous, I snapped a picture of Dante all chained up, his abs looking particularly defined in the position he was in, and sent it on to my best friend. Her response was instant. **Yes, please!!!**

I laughed, and when I looked up, was caught giggling by Dante. "You want me to tie you up later?" he asked me, just quiet enough that Soomi didn't hear, but not quite quiet enough for Jun not to hear.

"I am down for that!" Jun agreed.

Dante leaned over and smacked him upside the head. "Good, then I'm tying you to the bed in the villa. You can stay here while we go back to Seoul."

I laughed, moving out of the way so Soomi could get started.

## *H3RO*

Unlike the last shoot, there wasn't a cloud in the sky. It was hot and humid with little breeze in the old buildings. Although everyone was finding the shoot hard because of it, no one complained, instead cheering each other on. Once more I was insanely proud of H3RO and the crew, and the whole level of professionalism they provided.

I would have liked to have Kate there again, taking more behind the scenes shots, but she'd had a commitment back in Vegas and hadn't been able to make it. She had promised that with enough notice, she would be there for the next set of comeback photos though, and I had Jun armed with his camera helping me out.

By the time we got back to the villa in the early evening, everyone was ready for bed. Unfortunately, we only had a couple of hours before we were due at the resort owner's twin's seventeenth birthday party.

Jae and his team stuck around to help us get performance ready, and then we were picked up and taken to the main resort. The resort owner, Hong Changseok, was there to meet us. "Thank you so much for agreeing to do this," he said. "And thank you so much for all your hard work these last ten days. I've already seen some of the proofs of the shots, and H3RO have done a fantastic job. I'm proud to have them promoting my resort."

"Thank you so much for your kind words," I told him, swelling with pride.

"I will be passing these praises on to Lee Sejin too," he added. "He was so set on tweaking that contract to protect my resort, but there has been nothing of concern here."

I forced the smile to stay on my face even though Hong Changseok's words had me seething internally. There it was: confirmation that Lee Sejin had once again tried to screw with H3RO.

"If I could ask two last favors of you all?" Hong Changseok requested. I nodded. "My sons do not know that H3RO are still here and performing tonight. Would you remain in here until the performance?"

"Of course," I agreed. "But we would have done that anyway."

"Which leads me to my second request: Jun is something of a role model to Hong Wonseok. Would it be possible for him to perhaps meet with Jun?" he asked.

"H3RO are more than happy to take a couple of photos with both of your boys," I replied. "I'm sure there will be an opportunity for Jun and Hong Wonseok to talk too."

Hong Changseok disappeared leaving the seven of us alone in the large room that had been prepared for us. As far as green rooms went, this was one of the most luxurious. Minutes later, there was another knock at the door and a waitress entered carrying several trays of fresh, homemade pizza. My stomach grumbled in appreciation as I took a slice.

I wandered over to Jun who was chatting with Dante. "Could you make the time to chat with one of the twins—Hong Wonseok? He's a big fan of yours."

"Why?" Dante asked, rolling his eyes.

"Because of my good looks and exceptional vocals," Jun retorted. "Clearly he has taste."

"I don't know about that," Dante muttered. Then his eyes lit up. "Actually, let them meet. Then he'll be able to see what a fool he is."

Laughing, I moved round to Minhyuk. He was stretched out on a couch taking selfies. He smiled when I perched down next to him. "I'm just posting in our fan cafe," he told me.

"I wasn't checking up on that," I assured him. I

reached over to pat his thigh beside me, then left my hand there. "I just wanted to see how you were doing."

"I plan on sleeping all the way home," he said, then sighed. "Or I would if my name was Jun and I was capable of sleeping anywhere. Much as I've loved and appreciated this comeback, I am looking forward to some sleep. Although I'm going to have to clean our dorm before I do that."

I arched an eyebrow at him. "Really?"

"Oh, I guarantee you, Minhyuk will have unpacked his suitcase and will have all the clothes washed before you've gotten through the door. Then he'll clean the kitchen he left spotless, and then, because Jun's suitcase won't have moved from beside the door, he'll unpack that too," Nate declared, sitting beside me.

"I'm not that bad!" Jun objected from the other side of the room.

Dante smacked him upside the head. "Don't lie to Holly."

There was another knock at the door, and I stood, just as one of the resort staff walked in. "If you would like to follow me, it's time for your performance."

We did as requested and followed the man to the area the party was being held. In the center of the resort was a large swimming pool. Over the top. At one end a stage had been constructed. While the guests were enjoying themselves in and around the pool area, two boys were performing a cover of Shinhwa's 'This Love'.

While H3RO were busy with their pre-show ritual, I moved to the side to watch them. They were twins of high school age. They had the whole pool area, including me, entranced as I watched them. The song was about five years old, and I'd seen the video to it many times. These boys had taken the choreography and adapted it to fit the duo from the six piece it had been. On top of that, the two of them could sing—one of them in particular was belting out the high notes.

"They're good," Minhyuk said, joining my side.

Nate nodded. "Who are they?"

"I think they're the guys whose birthday it is," I said, uncertainly. The only idol twins I could think of were Kwangmin and Youngmin from Boyfriend, and Daeryong and Soryong of TASTY—and these two weren't either of them. However, they also looked nothing like the boys I'd seen in Hong Changseok's photograph.

"If they're not signed to an agency, you want to snap them up," Nate added.

"You're telling me," I agreed: the idea had already been in my head.

When their performance ended, the place went mad with applause and cheers. An MC walked on stage thanking the twins: they *were* Changseok's boys. Then he introduced H3RO. I knew instantly which twin was which when Wonseok saw Jun.

H3RO performed 'Who Is Your Hero?' as well as 'My Treasure', the album song they had created their own video for on the island. I was impressed with Wonseok and Wooseok who were singing and dancing along at the side of the stage.

Once the performance was over, and H3RO and the two boys were backstage chatting, I waited for an opportunity to speak to Wonseok, telling him that if singing was a career he or his brother were considering, to get in touch. I felt like a scout at a football game, and while I wasn't entirely sure what the criteria was for being on the Atlantis Entertainment roster, I would have been a fool not to get them to Seoul for an audition.

I was certain I would be seeing them again in the near future.

Eventually, our time was up. We were taken back to the villa for our final night. After the performance, and after such a hectic week, the guys all disappeared to their rooms for a shower and an early night. I couldn't say I blamed them. I however, opted for grabbing a bottle of water and made my way out onto the patio to sit on the swing seat.

I was looking forward to getting back to Seoul and for things to return to normal. I also really wanted to get Kyun back to the psychiatrist. He'd only had a handful of visits before we had flown out here, and I knew enough to know consistency was key.

I sighed, leaning back against the seat back, using my legs to set it swinging. Much as this place was a paradise, I was ready to leave.

"May I join you?"

"Always," I said, looking over at Tae. He was still in the outfit he had performed in and he hadn't bothered to take any of his makeup off either. "Is everything OK?" I asked as he sat down beside me. This was the first time he'd approached me since we had arrived here, and I couldn't help but feel nervous about whatever it was he was going to say.

"Kyun spoke to me," he said, quietly.

"Oh," I said, before chewing at my lip. I wasn't surprised, but it still wasn't helping with my nerves. For some reason, it felt like my boyfriend was about to break up with me.

"Holly, I know what I said, but I want to make sure, is this really what you want?" His expression was serious, as always, but I could see his dark eyes searching mine in the dim light.

"All I really know is how I feel about all of you," I told him. "And that is that I love you all."

Tae exhaled a long, deep breath. "Do you realize how impossible this is?" he asked me, sadly. "We all have a no-dating clause in our contracts, and even if we didn't, we couldn't really be public about it. For every person out there who would be happy about any of H3RO having a girlfriend, there would be two who would be against it."

"I know," I agreed, quietly.

"And that's if it's just one of us," he continued. "But six of us? At once?"

I turned to him, bringing one of my legs up underneath me. "I didn't expect this to happen when I became your manager, and honestly, I have no idea how this will work—if it *can* work—because I hear exactly what you're saying. I have thought about this a lot," I told him. "I've thought about how I'm older than half of you; how I'm your manager; how I'm not even a full Korean … Trust me, Tae, I haven't stopped thinking about this. And that's why I'm not prepared to let anyone try this unless they want to. Everyone has a lot to lose."

"But what if I don't go for it?"

I'd be heartbroken.

Before I could tell him that, he shrugged. "This does affect all of us—even those of us not involved. If this leaks, that's H3RO's reputation and our future gone. Regardless of who was involved and who wasn't."

"What are you saying, Tae?" I asked him.

He stared at me for the longest time, then shrugged. "I don't know," he admitted.

# 제13 장

# *H3R오*

*Lucifer*

Thanks to Inhye who had brought my tablets with her when she'd come to Jeju, the flight back to Incheon wasn't as bad as the flight to Jeju Island. We arrived back at the dorm before lunchtime, grabbing some sandwiches on the way. "I have good news," I announced to the table as we sat eating. "Short of the fan meeting we rescheduled from last week, Inhye has cleared your schedule. You guys have the next few weeks off, and we'll make sure you can all get out to visit your families. Even you, Nate."

Nate's eyes widened. He had been telling me that in the six and a half years since his debut, he'd only been home to San Francisco to visit his family once. "Really?" he asked.

I nodded. "Just let me know when you want to go and come back, and we'll organize it with Inhye," I told them. I was planning on heading back to Chicago to visit my mom too. As the table exploded into excited chatter, sandwiches almost forgotten about, my phone started ringing.

I stared at the name I had assigned the contact:

*Demon-spawn.*

I set my sandwich down, then stepped away from the table to take the call in my bedroom where it was quieter. "What?" I answered in greeting.

"It's Lee Sejin," he said.

"I know."

"And that's how you choose to greet me?"

"Yes," I agreed. "Because the way I'd rather greet you isn't suitable for minors and I don't want to risk getting into bad habits when I'm likely to be around underage fans on a regular basis. It wouldn't look good for Atlantis."

"Just get your annoying ass to Atlantis, now. And bring that financial drain of a group with you." Then he hung up on me.

While I appreciated technology, there were days that I wished we could go back in time, to just before cell phones, when everyone still had a phone with a wire attaching it to the wall. Aside from the fact it would have been harder for him to annoy me, it also would have left me the satisfying option of slamming the phone down. As it was, my new iPhone was too precious to launch across the room—not when H3RO's life and schedule was on it.

I returned to the kitchen, my appetite gone, and walked back to the table. "Guys, I need you to hold off your planning for a couple of hours," I told them, regretfully.

"You mean I can't go home?" Nate asked, his eyes wide once again, though this time at the idea of having the vacation taken away from him.

I shook my head. "I mean your planning. The demon-spawn wants to see us all, and I'm sure it's to congratulate us on wrapping up a successful comeback," I added, dryly.

They all looked as skeptical as I felt. No doubt there was something we had managed to do wrong, and I had a feeling the topic would probably revolve around Dani. The guys had already finished their sandwiches so I called for the minibus and less than an hour later, we were waiting in a conference room.

Dante and Nate were deep in conversation about vacation plans involving other countries. Jun, despite having a good night's sleep, was asleep in his chair, snoring gently. Minhyuk was wandering around the room, staring at the various album covers on the wall. Kyun and Tae were by the window though neither of them seemed to be talking.

I, meanwhile, was busy sending messages to Inhye to see if she had any idea what this meeting was about. She didn't.

Needless to say, my concern was growing, and it didn't get any smaller when Lee Sejin walked in with my father. Dante leaned over to Jun, smacking his shoulder to wake him. Jun's eyes shot open, ready to snap at Dante, when he spotted my father and stood. Thanks to Dante, he was on his feet only moments after the other members.

If it had been just Sejin, I would have remained seated, but seeing as I was trying to make an effort with Woojin, I stood too. We all waited for him to take his seat at the head of the table. While the others waited for Sejin to sit too, I didn't.

"Thank you all for coming," Sejin said as he sat. I folded my arms and stared at him, not buying his sickly-sweet greeting. "I understand you've been to Jeju

Island's Nirvana Resort."

There was so much I wanted to say to that, but I refrained. Not because I didn't want to upset him, but because I didn't want him taking his irritation out on H3RO *again*.

"I also understand you are now planning your vacation time."

How did he know that already? "Yes," I agreed. "I would think it was well earned, wouldn't you agree?"

"Perhaps," Sejin said, dismissively. "However, I would think you might want to reconsider that."

"Not really," I shrugged. "Like I said, it was well earned."

"You are aware that we are now six months away from H3RO's contracts expiring, correct?" he pressed on. "It is very soon that we would be entering into negotiations with you to renew those contracts."

"And?"

"I wish to make it very clear to you all right now, that unless you provide Atlantis Entertainment with that second number one you promised, there will not be any contracts renewed at all."

I let out a growl of frustration. "Oh, so what?" I asked, finally losing my patience. The group looked at me in alarm. "Don't renew their contracts."

"Holly!" Kyun exclaimed, looking terrified at the prospect.

"Kyun, being free of your contract means you could go elsewhere together." I would hate for them to go, but if it meant they would be able to get the career they deserved, I wouldn't hold them back.

They looked at each other, their eyes widening. The glimmer of hope was cut short by Sejin. "I can see from your expressions that you think that would be an easy option, which makes me think you've already forgotten the contracts you signed six and half years ago."

"What about them?" Tae asked, serious as ever.

"They all have a clause whereby, if Atlantis chooses to terminate them, or not renew, then you will not be able to sign for another agency for another five years," Sejin explained with a twisted grin on his face.

"You're an asshole," I blurted out before I could stop myself.

"Actually, that asshole would be father," Sejin corrected me. "He was the one who had it written to every Atlantis Entertainment contract."

"It protects the company," Lee Woojin agreed, somehow calmly.

"Speaking of protecting the company, I think we should also address how your behavior has been encouraging women like Min Dani," Sejin pressed on.

"Get out," I said, calmly.

"I'm not going anywhere," Sejin snapped at me.

"Good," I agreed. "But I'm not talking to you." I turned to H3RO. "I want all of you to go wait for me in my office."

"Holly—"

"Now," I cut Tae off.

Although confused, the guys did as I requested, leaving me alone with my father and half-brother. "None of those guys did anything wrong," I told them. "Not a single one of them did anything that encouraged that kind of behavior, and I will be damned if I'm going to let them sit there and listen to you say otherwise," I growled at Sejin. "Min Dani stole my luggage and Jun's luggage. She broke into a resort, impersonated an employee, and attempted to kidnap Jun. I dread to think what she would have done if I hadn't pulled her off him."

"Nate was all over her in a club, acting indecently," Sejin retorted.

"No!" I barked at him. "She stuck a roofie in his drink. That is not the behavior of someone sane, and there is nothing that anyone could do to encourage that kind of behavior, much less ask for it." As I glowered at him, I realized that I needed to add another item to the long list of things I needed to check on to see how much damage Sejin had done: check on the two girl groups on Atlantis' roster. If this was how he was with the male idols, I was terrified at what he had been doing to the females.

"Dani wasn't a fan," I continued. "She was a sasaeng and not only are they horrifying, but Atlantis Entertainment shouldn't be saying otherwise. I don't want anyone out there thinking this is acceptable behavior: someone could get hurt."

"Oh, stop being melodramatic," Sejin sighed, impatiently.

"Sejin, Holly is right," Woojin said, finally speaking up. "We have an obligation to look after the physical wellbeing of our artists."

"And the emotional wellbeing," I added.

Woojin nodded. "If we want them performing, we need them in good health. Sasaengs have hurt idols before."

I stood up, resting the palms of my hands on the table. "I'm done now."

"Holly, whether you like it or not, if H3RO want

to stay as H3RO, or continue as idols, they need to get that second number one. You might not have been clear with the timelines, but H3RO's contract takes all questions out of it," Sejin said, stopping me before I could storm out of there.

I rolled my eyes. "And am I going to find that every songwriter and recording studio is booked up for the next seven months?" I asked, dryly.

"I have arranged for some songs from our top writers to be left on your desk for you and H3RO to listen to," Woojin answered for him. "There will also be ample time available for recording, as well as a budget."

I walked out of the room and got halfway down the corridor, before I turned and kicked the wall. "Goddamnit!" I yelled.

"Holly?" It was my other brother with two guys about his age. Both of them looked alarmed at my outburst.

"Hi Seungjin," I sighed, rubbing at the back of my neck, awkwardly. There weren't many people who knew who I was, and I only vaguely recognized the two boys with him. They were in Bright Boys with him, but I couldn't remember their names. "I apologize. I'm just having family drama."

"We're here to talk to my brother about Bright Boys," Seungjin explained, giving me a pointed look.

"I'm sorry, but I'm trying to manage H3RO at the moment," I snapped at him. "I don't have time to save another group." I carried on down the corridor, then stopped. There was absolutely no need for me to have been so mean to Seungjin. It wasn't his fault his brother was being an ass, and I certainly had no right to use Bright Boys as a weapon: I wasn't Sejin.

I turned, hurrying back, ready to apologize. He was gone. I pulled out my phone and tapped out a quick message: **I was out of order, I'm sorry. Let me set up something with you and Bright Boys next week. I can't make any promises, but I will see what I can do.**

When I didn't get a response, I slipped my phone back into my purse and continued to my office.

Inhye was outside looking concerned. "H3RO are in your office."

"I know," I nodded. "I sent them in there."

"Why do they look like they've got months left to live?"

I sighed, running my hand through my hair. "Because that's exactly how Lee Sejin made it sound. Can you do me a favor and see if the retreat is free? And if so, can you arrange for that recording studio out there to be kitted out, ASAP."

"Of course," Inhye agreed. "How soon do you need it?"

I glanced at my office door, hating myself as I replied. "Today." Even Inhye looked disappointed for them. "And if you could make it so no one knows, that would be appreciated. I have no idea how the fans seem to know where we are all the time, but if I can't give them a real vacation, I would like to try to give them some privacy."

"We publish it," Inhye said with a frown. "It's standard policy for Atlantis as Lee Sejin likes the artists to have a crowd at the airports and for promotional activities. It makes the groups look popular."

We didn't have an inside leak—we just leaked it ourselves? I wasn't going to question it. If I thought about it, it was probably a good thing, and if nothing else, having a crowd was better than not having a crowd, but I was too pissed off at Sejin to be nice to him. "Don't publish it this time," I said. "Let us have some peace."

Inhye nodded, then I sucked in a deep breath and went into my office to break the bad news. No sooner had I stepped in, did my phone bleep. Ignoring the six members who had their eyes on me, I pulled out my phone, just in case it was Sejin delivering more crappy news.

It was Seungjin: **Don't bother.**

I sighed.

"Is everything OK?" Minhyuk asked.

I shook my head. "I was an ass to my brother."

"Good!" Jun cried.

"Wrong brother," I said, with another sigh. I slipped my phone into my pocket and joined them around my desk. "I'm sorry for kicking you all out like that," I apologized. "Everything that happened with Dani, and every other sasaeng or anti-fan you guys have, is not your fault and I didn't want you to hear any of that crap from Sejin. Just because that asshole believes it's all your fault, doesn't mean Atlantis does." I gave them a small smile. "Lee Woojin doesn't believe it either, for the record."

"What's happening, Holly?" Kyun asked. When I first met H3RO he had been convinced I was here to disband them and had walked around for weeks with a look of betrayal and desperation. While I was thankful the betrayal wasn't there, the desperation had returned.

"It's up to you," I told them all. "I will get Yongdae to look over the contracts, but I believe what

Sejin was saying. My father wouldn't have sat there and let him lie about that. However, I say this as your friend—not as your manager, and not as a lawyer—but given how this company has treated you, you might have grounds to get this taken to court. I can't say I'd blame you if you wanted to walk away from this."

Dante looked at the others, then shook his head. "We're H3RO. If we go anywhere else, we won't be. We've gotten a number one single once, and we can do it again."

I sagged, slumping against the desk. "I'm sorry: you wouldn't have to do it again if it wasn't for me saying I could get you two number ones."

Jun stepped forward, wrapping an arm around my shoulder. "Holly, we wouldn't have a number one at all if you hadn't come in and fought for us. We're in a much better position than we were a few months ago."

"Jun's right," Nate agreed.

"For once," Dante muttered under his breath, though he was grinning.

"Hey!" Jun objected.

"But he is right," Tae said, folding his arms. "We have gotten through so much, I don't think we should give up just yet. I've still got the fight in me."

"Have you got a song in you too?" Kyun asked.

Tae nodded. "Yes."

I smiled. We might have access to the best songwriters Atlantis had, but we weren't going to need them. "I'm sorry about your vacation plans," I told them.

"Mom never knew I was coming back, so she can't be disappointed," Nate shrugged.

"But you can be," I pointed out.

"And I am," Nate agreed with a nod of his head. "But all it does is make me more determined to show Sejin what I—what H3RO—is made of. Mom sent me here to follow my dreams. I'm not letting your brother stop them."

I held my hands up. "FYI, let's not refer to Sejin as my brother, please. I prefer the term, half-demon-spawn. Or asshole. Both have a nicer ring to them." I said, giving them a wry smile. "It's not a vacation, but Inhye is going to get us back at the retreat, only this time, there will be equipment in that studio. Lee Woojin also assured me we have a budget this time, so we don't have to worry about that. We also have recording studio time, and producers."

"Actually," Minhyuk piped up. "I know it's a lot of extra work, but I'd like to do the KPopKonneKt again. Not because of the money, although I wouldn't complain if we had something to fall back on if Lee Sejin decides to change his mind, but because it would be nice for the fans."

"That isn't what you were saying when you had hand cramp after signing all those albums last time," Nate joked.

Minhyuk nodded. "And I will probably have a hand cramp again, but I would like the opportunity to say thank you, and if this is the last chance we have, I want to take it."

The group fell into a somber silence, then Kyun nodded. "That would be nice."

Jun shook his head. "Don't say that like it's a done deal. With Tae, Dante and Minhyuk writing our songs, Nate on the choreography, Kyun's good looks, and my charming personality, we can do this again. We won't just be thanking them for the last seven years of support, but asking them to continue to support us for the next seven. Tae's right. Look how much we've been through. We can do this. We're H3RO!"

There was a moment's pause, and then Dante smacked Jun upside the head.

"What was that for?" Jun demanded.

Dante shrugged. "Sorry, that was habit."

"But Jun is right," Nate agreed. "We've got this."

I believed them.

It just wasn't going to be easy.

# 제14 장

# *H3RO*

*Easy Love*

I sent the group back to the dorm to pack. There were still a few things I needed to clear up with my father, and I also needed to talk with Inhye. Figuring the conversation with Lee Woojin was going to be the shorter of the two, I went to his office first.

"Holly," he greeted me, warmly.

"How long do we have, really?" I asked him, getting straight to the point. "Sejin said six months, but frankly, I don't trust him."

"You need time for negotiations," Lee Woojin told me with a shake of his head. "These don't happen overnight, especially if not everyone in the group wishes to renew their contract."

I pulled a face. H3RO had fought so hard to be here, I didn't want to consider that option. "Then what are you saying?"

"Normally, I would suggest three months, but that would put the comeback date in December."

"That's a problem?" I asked. Was Christmas an issue? South Korea didn't celebrate Christmas in the same way America did.

"Onyx are having a comeback at the beginning of December. I don't want two groups in our company competing against each other, but seeing as Onyx are a more popular group than H3RO, I don't want to jeopardize their chances."

I puffed out my cheeks, knowing that Sejin probably would have gotten me to agree to a December comeback without knowing that piece of information. I was glad I had come to Woojin. "But if we need time to negotiate contracts, and it's going to be about a month of promotions, you're saying that H3RO need to have their comeback in November?" I asked, doing the math in my head.

Woojin nodded, before clicking at something on his computer. "Onyx's comeback is scheduled for December fifteenth; that's not been officially announced, by the way," he added. "The latest H3RO should be aiming for is November thirteenth."

"That gives us the same amount of time as we had for the last comeback," I grunted.

"You did it once," Woojin shrugged.

I left him, irritable. OK, so maybe things were a bit easier this time around, and yes, it had been me who had promised that there would be two number ones, but honestly, he could have just voided that and renewed the contracts now. Why did they have to wait until the time was up?

I walked back to my office more determined than I had ever felt. It wasn't just that I wanted H3RO to succeed, but *I* wanted to succeed. Up until moving out here, I had never, *ever* considered a career in anything vaguely resembling the music industry. Now, I was set on becoming the Vice Chairwoman just so Atlantis had someone to call Sejin out on his bullshit treatment of the artists signed here. I might not have the industry experience or the business knowledge, but I could see when people were being mistreated and set up to fail.

The longer I was here, the more I knew what happened in Atlantis wasn't even unusual for the K-Pop industry. My hands curled into fists. Damnit, if I ended up being the only person in the company who acknowledged the idols as people instead of commodities, I was going to be that person.

"The retreat is all yours," Inhye told me as I walked to her desk. "And I have equipment being delivered first thing tomorrow morning. I assume you're heading out there today?"

I nodded. "As soon as I've taken care of a few things here, I will head back to the dorms and get us to Chiaksan this evening." I perched on the edge of her immaculate desk. "Inhye, I'm going to need all the help I can get. Our next comeback needs to be released in the middle of November."

Inhye's mouth fell open as she glanced at the calendar on her desk. "That's eight weeks."

"That's what we had for the last one too," I said, miserably. "I can't believe I put them in this position again."

"I was going to suggest coming with you, but I think in this instance, I would be better suited staying and taking care of as much as possible here."

I nodded. "I need an appointment made with Woo Byungho at KPopKonneKt as soon as possible."

"KpopKonneKt?" Inhye repeated in dismay. "Again?"

I held a hand up. "We have a budget, that's not a

problem. H3RO *want* to do it this time, for their fans. But we need to move quickly so it can be set up with time for people to contribute."

"I also want to make sure that the physical copies are distributed correctly this time. Sejin blocked that last time, and I know it had an effect on sales. Plus, we need recording studios booked."

"You also need Soomi back to finish off that video," Inhye added, already taking notes. "Leave it with me, Holly." She glanced at something on her computer, and then frowned. "What about the fan meeting you have booked for tomorrow?"

"Ah, crap!" I exclaimed. "I had forgotten about that. We're not cancelling: we've already rescheduled it once, and it's not fair for the fans. We'll do that, then head out to the retreat afterwards."

"You think you have time for a fan meet?" Sejin's voice boomed across the room. "Just because you managed to get a number one last time doesn't mean you'll get it this time."

I rounded on him, narrowing my eyes at him. "Is that a threat?"

"Pfft," Sejin scoffed. "I don't need to threaten you with anything." He pointed at Inhye. "You, on the other hand."

I stepped in front of her. "Park Inhye works for me now, not you, so don't you dare threaten her because I will take appropriate action against you."

"Look at you trying to be all intimidating," he mocked, stepping up to me, his tall lanky frame towering over me. "The fact is, Holly, in six months' time, H3RO will be no more, and when they leave, so will you. This company is about to undergo a good cleanout, and Inhye won't be the only one to be kicked out of the door."

I folded my arms and glowered up at him. "Who else are you threatening?"

"I'm not threatening anyone," he said with a dismissive wave of his hand. "I am going to remove the deadweight and troublemakers from this company. We don't need any more money drains here." With that, he turned and left, but not before I caught him muttering something about Bright Boys.

As soon as he was out of earshot, I turned to Inhye. "Get me everything you can on Bright Boys, and schedule a meeting with them for me some time in the next couple of weeks."

"Holly, do you have time to be saving another group?" Inhye asked, warily.

"Honestly, I don't know what the situation is with them," I replied. "But I at least want to see what is going on there before he can attempt to destroy another innocent group."

## H3RO

The members of H3RO were already packed and waiting for me when I arrived back at the dorm. I gave them an apologetic smile. "We're heading out there tomorrow now," I told them. "I rescheduled your last fan meet to tomorrow and I don't think it's fair to push that back again."

"Absolutely not," Tae said, voicing the agreement of the others who were nodding.

"But that doesn't mean we can't start now," Dante piped up. "We can head to the music rooms downstairs," he added, looking at Tae and Minhyuk.

"I want to come," Kyun added, quietly.

There was the briefest flash of surprise, but Dante wrapped his arm around the younger member. "Of course."

Tae looked to Nate and Jun. "What about you two?"

"I remember how this went last time," Jun shrugged. "I'm going to come up with ideas for the KpopKonneKt." Then his eyes widened. "But I'm coming with you, because you need a photographer."

"I don't think we do," Kyun grumbled.

"Actually, that's a good idea," I said. "Get teasing."

The group headed out of the door. I watched them go with a small smile. Last time, I had come back to them calling each other and themselves talentless, and here they were going out together, unprompted, and in higher spirits. It was a good sight to see.

I turned to grab my things: I was going to sit up on the roof and get started on the enormous task list I had, when I realized Nate was still here. "Is everything OK?" I asked him.

"Can I use your iPad?" he asked as he rubbed at the back of his neck. "It's just, I thought I would be seeing my parents, and now I'm not, I've realized how long it's been since I spoke to them."

"Of course," I said, pulling it out of my purse and handing it over. "Nate, I'm really sorry I got your hopes up about this, but I promise, even if I buy you that ticket personally, I will make sure you see your parents."

"It's not your fault," he told me. "I'll be OK. I just want to see how they're doing." I knew that wasn't true, but Nate had already walked off towards his room.

With him using the iPad, I went to my room to collect my laptop, then went upstairs to the roof. I deposited the laptop on the seats up there, then went to the edge of the building so I could look out over the city.

Standing back there gave me a weird feeling. So much had changed, and yet so much had remained the same. In some ways, H3RO were in a much better place. They had a number one single and they had the knowledge that they had accomplished that without any help. They were tougher than they were and their friendship was stronger than ever—even with me in the equation.

But on the flip side, we were back at square one, working our asses off to get an album together in almost the same timespan as we had last time. Even though there were six months left on their contracts, time needed to be factored in for negotiations. These things didn't happen overnight, and there were six people to take into account. Would they all want to stay? Would they all want to continue with music? Tae was coming close to mandatory enlistment age. I'd seen so many groups unable to survive the enlistment period. I knew what Tae had said about H3RO, but that didn't mean his opinion wouldn't change.

My phone beeped at me and I glanced at it, seeing an email from Inhye with a collection of attachments. Instead of attempting to read them on my phone, I returned to the laptop, pushing those negative thoughts from my head. Doubting Tae—or any of H3RO—was the last thing I should be doing right now.

I stretched out, the laptop on my lap, and started

reading through the dozens of emails Inhye was sending through. Most related to H3RO's comeback, and I found some of the tension I'd been carrying ease up a little knowing Inhye was on the case. A couple of other emails related to Bright Boys. Instead of reading them, I filed them into another folder until I had the time to read through what I was sure was going to be a wormhole of misinformation and opinion.

"Why do you always come up here without a drink?" Nate asked as he thrust a bottle of water in between my face and the laptop screen.

I took it from him and shrugged. "I get distracted by work," I told him. "But thank you."

He sat down beside me. "I guess it gives me an excuse to see you."

"You don't need to bring me water to find a reason to see me," I laughed. "Just come see me."

Before I could say anything else, he suddenly reached out and pulled me into his lap. I had to shoot one hand out to grab the laptop, and the other away from me to stop from spilling the water everywhere. "Good," he murmured in my ear as his arms tightened around my waist.

I pushed the laptop to one side, then turned in his lap so I could see him. "How's your mom?"

"Missing me," he said, sadly. "I shouldn't have called. It only upsets her."

"I disagree," I told him. "No matter how much she misses you, she's always going to want to hear from you."

"That's what she said," he sighed. "And then she burst into tears." He leaned back into the seat, bringing me with him. "She read the Dispatch articles."

"I spoke to my mom when we were in Jeju," I admitted. "She'd seen the same ones. She was ready to come over and beat your ass." As Nate's eyes went wide, I giggled. "Don't worry; I set her straight."

I leaned over to set the water bottle down on the ground. When I returned to an upright position, I found Nate's eyes staring intently on my face. Slowly, his hand came up to my cheek, gently brushing over it with his fingertips. "It has gone now, hasn't it?"

I nodded. "The makeup isn't covering that bruise up anymore. It's gone," I assured him.

"I really am sorry about that," he said, hanging his head.

I reached up, tilting his head to mine. "The person whose fault it is, was arrested, remember?" Gently, I pulled him to me, then captured his lips with my own. I could feel his smile against my mouth, then his lips were tugging at mine.

While our tongues played with each other, my hands ran down his neck and over his chest. One of Nate's hands stayed around my waist, keeping me in place, while the other descended down my leg, massaging my thigh. As our kisses became more intense, his hand trailed under my skirt, skimming over the top of my panties.

It was the lightest of touches, but it had heat radiating everywhere, and I couldn't stop the gasp of anticipation. The noise had Nate's hand shooting out from under my skirt, but only so he could put his hands on my waist and lift me so I was straddling him, a knee either side of his hip.

"Oh, hell," I groaned, feeling his erection pressed up against me.

His eyes heavy with lust, locked on mine. He reached up, unbuttoning my blouse, until he could push it down my arms. Then his gaze fell on my shoulders with a small frown. "Is that Kyun again?" he asked.

I glanced down at the small collection of bite marks and hickeys. "Yes," I said, softly. "Does that bother you?"

He looked up at me and slowly shook his head. "I think it amuses me more than anything. I really didn't take Kyun to be a biter." Then he tilted his head. "Or is that what you like?"

"I didn't ask him to do that, if that's what you mean?" I told him, wondering why this conversation wasn't as uncomfortable as I thought it would be, even if it was a little weird. "And so long as he doesn't go much higher—at least in this heat—then I don't mind it. I don't think he realizes he's doing it," I added before I shrugged. "It's Kyun."

A small smile appeared on Nate's face. "Is it strange that we're having this conversation?"

"A little," I admitted. "But it's not awkward. At least it's not for me."

"No, I guess it's not for me, either," he frowned. "Maybe Jun was onto something." He met my gaze then arched an eyebrow. "I can't believe I said that, either."

"How about instead of bringing Jun into this conversation, we bring the focus back on you and me?" I leaned forward, grinding up against him. He let out a hiss, his hands shooting to my waist to hold me in place. I reached down for his hands, plucking them from my sides and moved them up to my breasts, then leaned over to kiss him again.

Nate didn't need telling twice. Our mouths

worked in sync, while I grinded against him.

And then my phone rang. I pulled back, glancing at the name, and then groaned—this time in displeasure. "It's Lee Woojin," I told him.

"Ignore it," Nate commanded, plucking it from my hand and dropping it on the couch. When he returned his hand to me, it was to my back to unclasp my bra.

The phone rang again.

"I'm supposed to be working," I pointed out, regretfully. "On your comeback."

Nate collapsed back into the couch, his head resting on the back. "I know," he muttered up to the roof of the structure we were under.

"Hello," I said, answering the phone. I listened to my father then frowned. "Just give me a minute," I requested, before muting the call. "This is going to be a long call," I told Nate.

Nate lifted his head, then sighed. "To be honest, my intention had been to bring you a drink and then go join the others. I just got distracted by your body." He stretched up, kissing me briefly, then offered a hand so I could slide off him. I quickly pulled my blouse on, not wanting to talk to my father without it on and gave Nate an apologetic smile. He stood. "Later," he promised, before walking off.

# 제15 장

# *H3RO*

## *Love Equation*

By the following evening, we had arrived at the company retreat. Everyone had reclaimed the rooms they had taken previously. We were all in the kitchen watching Minhyuk, who was still wearing a pair of bear ears that a fan had given him, and Dante cook jjajangmyeon. The smell of the black bean sauce was making my stomach grumble.

"Where did you learn to cook, Minhyuk?" I asked him.

"My family has a restaurant in Ulsan. I used to help my parents before I moved to Seoul," he told me.

"We visited once," Jun said, excitedly. He got up and started to pull glasses out of the cupboard to set on the table. "Minhyuk's dad makes the best hotteok."

"What's that?" I asked.

"Hotteok is hotteok," Jun shrugged.

Dante clipped him around the ear. "You can't describe something using the same word."

"Then you describe it!" Jun objected.

Dante opened his mouth and then stopped with a frown. "I only remember the Chinese word."

"Pancakes," Nate supplied, in English. "They're like little sweet pancakes with syrup inside."

Minhyuk shook his head. "My mom makes them. Dad makes noodles."

"And Minhyuk is the best cook in our dorm," Tae declared, making Minhyuk beam with pride.

Together, we carried the food and plates outside to the large outdoor table. Although it was late September, the weather was still warm. Without all the humidity we had experienced the last time we were here, it was pleasant to sit out in the late evening sun.

"Do you cook, Holly?" Minhyuk asked, curiously.

I shook my head. "My mom owns a Korean restaurant too, but you're talking to the girl who managed to ruin a week's worth of kimchi. I worked out front. Plus, it helped my mom out with the English."

"Then how do you not know what hotteok is?" Jun frowned, confused.

"More importantly, how do you ruin *kimchi*?" Kyun asked in horror.

I shrugged, sheepishly. "I put in vinegar instead of fish oil."

Six outraged faces stared at me. "Even I know that's wrong," Dante exclaimed.

"I'm better at western foods," I shrugged, dismissively. "So," I said, changing the subject before they discovered my 'western foods' really consisted of waffles and pancakes from store bought batter. "How did it go in the studio yesterday?"

"We're still trying to agree on a theme for the song," Tae replied.

I caught Nate and Jun sharing a look which told me that translated to 'not good'. "It's OK," I assured them. "I wasn't expecting you to create an album in a day. You have plenty of time."

"Holly, we have a couple of weeks," Tae corrected me, vaguely.

"But you're H3RO," I shrugged. "You did it once, and I know you can do it again."

"What if we can't?" Kyun asked, his expression going bleak.

"*Hyung*!" Jun exclaimed. "We can do it."

Kyun shook his head. "I'm serious. What if we can't do it?" I chewed at my lip and stared at him from across the table. I knew how desperately he wanted to believe they could do it, but I also knew a career of being put down by Sejin had almost destroyed any faith in himself he had left. "We all keep saying we're going to do it, but all we've been doing for the last six months is avoid talking about what happens if we don't. Lee Sejin has been set on disbanding us for years. What's to say that, even if we do get another miracle and another number one, he's not going to disband us anyway?"

"Me and my father," I told him firmly. I set my chopsticks down and walked around to his side of the table. I had been prepared to crouch down beside him, but Nate stood, vacating his seat for me. "Kyun, if you could do anything you wanted to, what would it be?" I asked him, softly.

"H3RO," he responded without even thinking about it. "H3RO's my life: my family."

"We're not going anywhere," I told him.

"Hell no," Dante agreed.

"You're stuck with us," Minhyuk added.

"Even me, because I'm not going anywhere either," Jun said, firmly.

Kyun rolled his eyes at that, but he shrugged. "It's not that." He rubbed at the back of his neck, awkwardly. "H3RO isn't just us. It's performing and being on stage. If we hadn't have had the last comeback, I maybe could have coped with that, but I remember what it's like to be on stage, that's fresh in my memory. I don't know anything else. I didn't finish school, and I wasn't good at it when I went." He looked at me, his eyes wide and brimming with tears. "If we don't make this happen, and Lee Sejin gets his way and disbands us, with that clause, we can't even go anywhere else and do this."

I slipped off the chair, dropping to my knees in front of Kyun so I could pull him into a hug. "We're going to do this."

Nate stepped forward, meeting my gaze as he clamped a hand on Kyun's shoulder. "We're not talking about other options, Kyunnie, because there are no other options. We've come this far because we believed in each other. Don't stop that now. Doubt will be the thing that stops us, not Lee Sejin."

I stepped back and gave Kyun a bright smile. "He's right."

Kyun nodded, then glanced over at Tae. "Are you going to add something sentimental to this?"

"It's not over until we say it's over," he told him. "Lee Sejin might think he controls our career, but we control our future."

## H3RO

I was left alone not long after that. The guys had decided they wanted to be in the studio working on the album, and I spent some time cleaning up after dinner. Not expecting to see them again, I retired to my room, taking a long shower, before curling up in my bed. It was time to tackle the Bright Boys problem, and that meant researching.

I lost track of time as I disappeared down the gossip and speculation black hole. The only facts seemed to be that the leader of Bright Boys, Park Hyunseo, had attacked a guy in a club, and somehow another member, one of the solo artists on the Atlantis roster and a non-idol friend who used to be an Atlantis trainee, had been caught up in it. None of them were talking. I had just dropped Inhye an email asking her to make a meeting with Hyunseo first, before I spoke to the rest of the group, when there was a knock at the door.

"Hello?" I called out.

Tae stepped into the room, closing the door behind him. He stood in front of it looking uncomfortable. "I didn't think you would be up still, but I saw your light on."

I glanced at my phone to check the time. It wouldn't be long before the sun would be up! "I lost track of time," I told him, surprised at myself. "What about you?"

"Same," he shrugged. He rubbed his hands on his sides. "Can we talk?"

I nodded, gesturing to the bed. "Always."

Hesitantly, he made his way over to the bed, perching on the edge of it. "In all the years I've known Kyun, he has never admitted what he's feeling to the group."

"He can come across as being very detached at times," I said, thoughtfully. "That being said, I don't

142

think he is. He just keeps his emotions and thoughts to himself most of the time."

"You don't understand," Tae said with a shake of his head as he turned to face me. "That has *never* happened. Whenever anything has ever upset him, he has always retreated off by himself. Whenever he gets stressed about it, he will get angry, but it's usually something else he's using as a cover. He has never admitted what has really upset him. I've always had to pry it from him."

I got out from under the covers and swung my legs around so I was sitting beside Tae. "He's been seeing a psychiatrist, don't forget," I pointed out.

"I don't think it's that," Tae disagreed.

I stared at him. "Don't you dare try and say it's me." Tae stared at me. "Tae!" I cried, jumping to my feet.

Tae was up in a shot in front of me, his hands gently grabbing my upper arms. "No, not completely," he said.

I could see he was searching for the words, but I shook myself free of his grip and folded my arms as I stared at him. "Tae, I am not responsible for that."

"I think you are, but not in the way you think you are," he finally told me. It didn't help with my confusion and I arched an eyebrow at him. "No matter what we've said or done, Kyun has never seen himself as our equal. Whenever we've been interviewed and asked who is the best at anything, he has never once said himself, but he's always the first to put himself down. He knows he has talent, he knows he can sing, and he knows how important he is to H3RO, but he has also confessed that there are times when he thinks H3RO would be able to survive without him, and our Treasures would get over him leaving."

I closed my eyes, rubbing at my forehead. "I'm going to kill Sejin, I really am."

"This goes back further than Atlantis," Tae said, sadly.

I looked up at him, remembering what he said about how he came to know Kyun, despite their age difference. I sighed. "I'm still going to kill him. He's not helped matters."

"But I do think you have," he repeated. Once again, he reached out for me, only this time I didn't move away. "This thing—this being with all of us … I … I think it's the first time Kyun has been shown that he is equal. There is no one from management ranking us, and there are no fans arguing over who is their bias. It is just you choosing us all."

I stared up at him, slowly shaking my head. Tae let go of me and walked away. "When I first heard you'd slept with Kyun, I was hurt. I thought we had something," he told me, without turning back to face me. "Then when Jun came out with this idea, before I could even think about it, Kyun was hurt because he thought you were choosing the others over him, that he was just a thing to pass the time."

"I have never thought that!" I objected almost vehemently. "Ever."

Tae finally turned back to me, nodding. "I know, but if you look at it from Kyun's point of view, where he's always comparing himself, you can see why he'd think that." He ran a hand through his hair as he raised his shoulder at me. "Then I was angry. I couldn't see how you could possibly like us all like that, much less want to be with us all. I was convinced you would pick one of us, and I was more terrified it wasn't going to be Kyun than me. When he found out about the others, about Nate, I thought he was going to quit right then. If we hadn't had to rush off to Jeju, I think he would have."

My stomach churned. I had done exactly what I'd never wanted to do and hurt any of them.

"I had a plan," Tae continued. "I was actually going to do my best to make sure that you picked Kyun. The rest of us, I know we could have handled it, but he wouldn't have. And then, whatever happened on Jeju happened."

I blinked. "He didn't tell you that?" I asked, surprised. I didn't think it was that significant that he couldn't have done. Tae shook his head. "Oh, well—"

"If Kyun didn't want to tell me, you don't have to," he said, cutting me off. "The point is, whatever happened, something changed." He walked back to me. "I didn't see it until this evening: what you said to Kyun, about us staying together … you meant it."

It wasn't a question, but I nodded anyway.

"Yes," he agreed. "Because Kyun believed it. And, so did I."

"You did?" I asked, surprised.

Slowly, Tae nodded. "I really do. And what's more, even though it's not going to be easy, I think it can work."

I couldn't help but stare up at him with skepticism. "You do?"

"I said I didn't think it would be easy," he shrugged. "But yes, I do. With all of us." I continued to stare up at him in disbelief. "Including me," he added.

"But what about what you said the other night?" I asked him. "Your no-dating clause, and H3RO's reputation?"

"I don't think it's going to be easy," he repeated once more. "But I think it's worth it." He gave me a sad smile. "Assuming we can survive your brother."

"H3RO is stronger than that asshole. Don't you start failing to believe in yourself now. You control your future, remember?" I stared up at him, hoping that he hadn't changed his mind from that earlier conversation, because if he was faltering, they all would. "Those guys need you to be strong so you can lead them—"

Tae stepped forward, his hand disappearing into my hair as he leaned over and kissed me. I reached up for him, my heart swelling as I wrapped my arms around his neck. I had grown to believe this would never happen again, that I would never feel his mouth on mine. I had been so convinced that he would never come to accept the idea of us all, that I couldn't get enough of him.

And then I pulled away, biting at my swollen lips as I stepped back from him. "Tae, are you really OK with this? Less than a day ago, you weren't, and you came in here telling me how you'd planned to convince me to pick one of you—if you think that's still a possibility—"

Without warning, Tae stepped forward. His movement surprised me and as I tried to move out of his way, I slipped backward. The next thing I knew, his arm shot out, grabbing me, pulling me towards him. I stared up at him, still hanging at an awkward angle even though I was safe in his arms. "I'm more than OK with this," he promised, before kissing me again.

I threw my hesitation to one side, believing in the unspoken words of his kiss. Then, as he pulled me upwards, I decided his clothes needed to join it. My hands reached for the bottom of his T-shirt, tugging it upwards. Tae stepped back, just enough to whip the shirt off, then his mouth was back on mine.

His kisses were almost as desperate as I'd felt; like he'd thought they were never going to happen again. I felt a franticness in me as I kissed him, like I couldn't get enough of him.

Tae pulled back, and I reached for his face, trying to bring him back to me, but his hands caught mine first. Breathing heavily, he leaned forward, resting his forehead against mine, but making sure I couldn't kiss him again. "Holly," he murmured. "Holly, I'm not going anywhere."

I closed my eyes, trying to push the strange, tense energy from me. "I don't know why I'm acting like this," I whispered.

Tae let go of me, but only so he could wrap his arms around me, holding me tightly against his hard, bare chest. As my ear pressed against his chest, his hands rubbed gently at my back. "I'm not going anywhere," he said again. I clung to him, listening to him repeat those words over again. Finally, he led me over to my bed, pulling back the covers. "I'm staying here tonight," he informed me. He let go and got in, shuffling over before reaching up and pulling me down beside him.

He leaned over to turn the lamp off and the room descended into darkness. "I'm sorry," I said, embarrassed by my actions. "I don't know what's wrong with me."

"There's nothing wrong with you," he assured me. He reached over, pulling me back to him, wrapping his arms around me.

I nestled into the crook of his arm. My hand, resting on his chest by my face, started tracing a pattern on his skin. "I thought Jun was crazy," I told him, quietly, trying to put what I was feeling into words. "And then the others started to agree with him, and I thought maybe … until you said …"

"Holly, I love you."

I shifted my head to look up at him, just making out his eyes shining in the darkness. "I love you," I responded as the last of the weird feeling left me. I could feel my body relax into his even as my skin seemed to hum in all the places it was touching Tae's.

# 제16 장

# *H3R오*

*Watch Out*

We lay there like that for a while, nothing but the sound of wind rustling in the trees from the open bedroom window, and our own breathing. At some point, Tae fell asleep, snoring softly.

For some reason, I couldn't sleep. I was comfortable and felt completely safe, but my mind wouldn't switch off. The worry and fear that had been lingering because of our personal situation had gone, and with it went the last of the knot of guilt in my stomach. However, the thought of how much work we had to do in such a short window of time for their comeback—the comeback that their careers were depending on—it just wouldn't allow me to switch off.

Instead of counting sheep, I was trying to create a mental list of everything we needed to do, despite the fact I had been doing that all day. Although that was written down and saved in the cloud, I was trying to think of anything I could have missed, or any idea that might help.

Eventually, I could feel myself nodding off … which was when there was a knock at my bedroom door. It was soft, but in the still of the night, loud enough to bring me back from that almost sleep state.

I rolled over in Tae's arms, trying not to disturb him, but his hold tightened. "Ignore it," he whispered, gruffly, still half asleep. He pulled me back so my back was flush with his chest, then let out a soft sigh as he fell back to sleep.

I lay there, staring at the door, waiting for another knock. There wasn't one. Just as I thought Tae's plan had worked, the door handle rattled, and then a head poked in.

"Holly?" Kyun's soft whisper seemed louder than it was.

"I'm awake," I responded as quietly as I could, hoping this didn't wake Tae either.

"Tae's still in the studio," he muttered, stepping into the room.

I froze, wondering what to do. Selfishly, I'd allowed Tae to stay, forgetting Kyun had trouble sleeping by himself. I jumped when Tae pulled his arm free and used it to lift the blankets. "Get in," he said, his voice still full of sleep.

"Tae?" Kyun question.

"Get in," Tae repeated, still holding the blanket up. "Holly's getting cold," he added as I shivered against him as a cool breeze blew over us.

There was only a moment's hesitation, and then Kyun crossed the room, getting in the bed on the other side of me. Tae dropped the cover over us, and after another pause, Kyun huddled into me, sandwiching me between the two of them.

I held my breath before I could stop myself. From around me, Tae's arm reached over me for Kyun, ruffling his hair. "No funny business," he warned him. His arm relaxed, draping over me. "Same goes for you," he added with a yawn.

I lay there, staring at Kyun who was facing me, his nose centimeters from mine. Behind me, Tae's breathing settled into a steady rhythm. "I'm sorry," I whispered. "I didn't mean to take him away from you.

Kyun leaned forward, lifting his head so he could tilt it slightly to kiss me. "I get both of you now." His lips barely touched mine before he pulled back. "I didn't mean it like that. Tae and I—"

"I know," I told him. "Not everything, but enough." When I sensed the discomfort coming from Kyun, I yawned loudly. "Well, I can't say I ever expected this," I murmured, changing the subject.

"Is this too weird for you?" Kyun asked me. "I can leave if you prefer," he said, starting to slide out of the bed.

I reached out and grabbed his hand. "It's OK," I assured him. "It's different, but it's absolutely OK."

He eased back but didn't let go of my hand, instead rubbing his thumb over the top of it. "That's a relief," he admitted.

## H3RⱣ

It was a feeling of being watched that woke me up. I was sprawled over Tae, with Kyun curled up into my back. I looked up, but Tae was still fast asleep. Trying not to disturb either of them, I rolled over as carefully as I could. Kyun rolled over himself, but he stayed asleep.

In between them both, I was hot. While I was

exceptionally comfortable, I needed to cool down. I was trying to work out the best way to extract myself when a gentle cough caught my attention.

I found Jun leaning against the wall by the door, his arms crossed and a large smirk on his face. "I came in to see if you knew where Tae and Kyun were. Apparently, you do."

"It's not what you think," I murmured, trying to keep my volume low, and equally feeling a little embarrassed.

"I think you're going to need a bigger bed," he declared as a giant grin appeared on his face.

"Oh, no," said, shaking my head at him.

Jun ignored me, darting over, then crawling up and lying down on me. His arms somehow got under the covers and around me. "You're comfortable," he whispered, settling his head on my chest. Then he propped himself upright, leaning over to kiss me. All of a sudden, two hands from either side of us shot up and smacked Jun upside the head. "Hey!" he objected, only just avoiding headbutting me.

"No funny business while we're in the same bed," Kyun grunted.

"What are you doing up anyway?" Tae asked. "You are aware there's an 'a.m.' after the number, right?"

I bit back a laugh—he had a point.

"That's not funny, hyung," Jun complained, sitting up so he was straddling me. "I came to see where you were, because yesterday you really wanted us to spend the day in the studio, so I set my alarm early to be there, only you weren't."

Tae frowned, looked at his watch, then swore

loudly. "I left my alarm clock in my room." He extracted his arm from under me and sat up, rubbing at his face. "Thank you for waking me up, Jun."

Jun blinked a few times, and then grinned. "Minhyuk is making breakfast." He leaned forward, kissed me, then bounded off the bed and out of the room.

I watched him go with a frown. "Is anyone else disturbed by the fact it's really early, and not only is Jun awake before us, but he's ridiculously happy."

"More than you know," Kyun grumbled. "I hope he's not going to be like that all day."

"You should know by now, if he wakes up with this much energy, he will be like that until he falls asleep," Tae sighed. He rubbed his hand over his face, then shook his head. "Come on, let's get breakfast, then get in the studio." He gave me a kiss, then got out of bed, stretching, as he was walked out of my room.

Instead of moving, Kyun snuggled up against me, tightening his grip. "I want to stay here instead."

Before I could agree with him, the door opened again, and Tae stuck his head back in. "Come on, Kyunnie," he called.

"I'm coming," Kyun grumbled in defeat. He got up off the bed, got halfway to the door, then hurried back to give me a kiss. Then, following after Tae, he left my room, closing the door behind him.

I lay back on my bed, staring up at the ceiling. "Well, this isn't going to take much getting used to," I told the ceiling fan.

I stretched out, then got up myself. As we were back in the cabin with no one but H3RO to see what I was wearing, I opted for a light summer dress. Today, my office was going to be the outside table, and seeing as though the guys were going to be locked in a studio all day, I was opting for the second-best view in the place: the pool.

By the end of the second week, I had barely seen any of H3RO. They had all but locked themselves away in the studio all day and most of the night. Nate would come out to check on me, bringing me drinks, and together, we would end up taking bottles through to restock the fridge in the studio. Or rather, I would get as far as the door and one of the others would take the bottles off me because I wasn't allowed to hear the demos until they had finished.

Minhyuk would appear less often than Nate, usually when someone remembered that they needed to eat. Lost in my own work, trying to make this album run as smoothly as possible, I wasn't great at remembering either. I did go out and get some groceries, but after a few failed attempts at cooking, and because the only things I did know how to cook were mainly meaty which didn't work for Kyun, a lot of take out was ordered and consumed in the studio. At least by the guys, because I was still banned from being in there.

After day four, and Kyun making a passing comment about how he was going to have to hit the gym for a couple of hours, I returned to the local village every other day to do some more grocery shopping. This time, I bought lots of fruit and vegetables for salad. My plan was to make up some meals for them, as I needed to head back to Seoul for a meeting with Bright Boys. I also needed to catch up with Inhye to see how things were going.

Finally, Tae had mentioned he was hoping to

produce the album himself again, rather than use one of the regular Atlantis producers, and I wanted to check if Youngbin was available to assist once more. They had worked well together last time, and if nothing else, it was only so Tae would have someone to bounce ideas off if needed.

I returned to the retreat to silence. I wasn't surprised as the guys were still in the studio. I had just finished bringing all the bags inside when I heard a noise upstairs. I glanced at the clock on my phone. It was late afternoon. Since we'd gotten here, the guys had been keeping odd hours. Although I wasn't keen on them working all day and night and not getting enough fresh air, I equally didn't want to disrupt their creativity.

I finished putting most of the groceries away, leaving out what I need for bibimbap. After a conversation with one of the elderly women, an ajumma, at the vegetable stall at the market, I had left with a recipe that she assured me I couldn't get wrong. Seeing as it required cooking fern, I wasn't sure about that, but it was something different to pizza and I wanted to try it.

I chopped the fern up while I heated the water, then threw it in to leave boiling. I had about twenty minutes before I needed to get the rice cooking, and I had a good idea of exactly what I wanted to do in that time.

I made my way upstairs, wanting to see who was up there as they hadn't come down yet, and more importantly, if they had any idea when they would break for dinner (although experience told me that I would end up bringing them food anyway). "Who's up here?" I called out, good naturedly as I walked up the stairs.

"And how much of a break do you have?" I added with a grin, sure I could convince whoever it was to stay in their bedroom a while longer.

Although I had shared a bed with a different member of H3RO each night, we had done nothing more than kissing. I was feeling up for a little more than a kiss, and I was hoping whoever was up there would feel the same way too.

All of a sudden, a blur of black charged towards me. There was just enough time for me to see that the figure wasn't one of H3RO, and they were hidden behind a mask and a cap. I couldn't see much more as they shoved me. My hands shot out, but not quick enough to grab at anything other than air. I fell backwards, landing heavily on the stairs. I let out a scream of pain as I continued rolling down the stairs, and then I came to an abrupt stop. The last thing I remember was staring up at the figure—a woman—before blacking out.

# 제17 장

# H3RO

*Oh My!*

"Someone call an ambulance!"

The yell woke me up, and I winced at the noise as it reverberated around my skull. "She's waking up!"

"Can we not yell?" I murmured as I opened my eyes and found two Minhyuks and two Dantes staring down at me. While they became singular figures, I quickly took stock of myself. My head hurt, and my back was sore, but I didn't think anything was broken. "And don't call an ambulance," I added, trying to sit up.

Minhyuk and Dante both shot forward. Dante was trying to help me up, whereas Minhyuk was trying to keep me lying down. "It's too late for that," Tae informed me, appearing in my peripheral. "The ambulance is on its way and you should stay still," he added, though I think the last part was aimed at Dante.

"Let me sit up," I said, shaking Minhyuk off me. He backed off, eyes wide and face pale. Ignoring his leader, Dante continued to help me up.

When the room swam again, I half wished I'd listened to Tae, as I let my head fall into my hands with a groan. "Did anyone catch her?" I asked, weakly.

"Catch who?" Kyun asked.

I opened my eyes, and carefully looked around. I was still at the bottom of the stairs; I guess they were too scared to move me. All six of them were stood or crouched around me, and all of them looked scared.

"You mean you didn't fall?" Dante asked.

I shook my head, and then instantly regretted it. I sucked in a deep breath and blew it out slowly, surprised at how nauseous I felt. Maybe a check with the doctor wasn't such a bad idea. "No, I was pushed," I explained. "I thought it was one of you upstairs, and when I went up, some girl came running at me."

"Who was she?" Tae asked, crouching down in front of me. "Did you see her?"

I was about to shake my head again, but stopped myself just in time. "She was wearing a mask and a cap. All in black too." I closed my eyes, partly because the room was spinning again, partly to try to conjure her image up in my head. "She had hair in a chin-length bob, and she was shorter than me," I told them. "She came out of one of the bedrooms, but she may have been in all of them. She was upstairs a little while at least, before I went up."

"You're not bleeding, but I think you hit your head pretty hard," Minhyuk told me.

"I can believe that," I agreed, leaning against Dante, who gingerly wrapped an arm around my shoulders to hold me upright. "You guys need to check your rooms."

"Right now, we need to make sure you're OK," Nate corrected me.

I tried to swallow back the fresh wave of nausea,

and then took another deep breath. "I'm not going to pretend I'm OK, because I hurt. A lot. *But*, someone broke into this place. We're going to need the police out here." That wasn't the whole reason. I wanted to know if she was here to rob the place, or because H3RO were here. My brain was telling me it had to be a coincidence; that she was here to steal from whoever happened to be her. No one knew we were here. I had made sure of that with Inhye.

But with everything that had happened with Nate, and again in Jeju, my gut was telling me I shouldn't rule anything out. Not when it came to H3RO's safety.

"I'll go check my room," Nate said, quietly. The look on his face told me he knew what I was thinking, but he hurried up the stairs without commenting. I stayed seated, leaning against Dante's hard chest, feeling strangely comforted by it. A short time passed, and Nate returned. "I can't tell if anything is missing," he admitted. "But someone had definitely been through my things."

I nodded, barely moving my head. My eyes closed, and the thought of sleep was appealing to me. Only, no sooner had I decided that a nap would help my headache, Minhyuk was gently shaking my shoulder. "You can't sleep," he told me.

I turned around and threw up, narrowly missing him.

"Where's that ambulance?" Jun cried.

"It's just vomit," Minhyuk told him, calmly. I caught him shoot Jun a look.

"I'm sorry," I said, meekly, trying to get up so I could clean the mess up. Dante's arm tightened around me, keeping me still.

"Stay put," Dante murmured at me.

I decided not to argue, feeling worse. I closed my eyes again.

## H3RO

Bed rest was boring.

After being admitted into the hospital and having a brain scan, I had spent a night in the hospital and then discharged. Tae had gone to the hospital with me and acted as my guardian until Lee Woojin had arrived.

That was a strange event. We still weren't close, and I still hadn't reached the point where I could call him dad (or any variation), but for the first time, I think it was fair to say, I felt genuine concern from him.

There were no flowers or chocolates, or even hugs, but he was there. I made him promise not to call my mom as it would only worry her. I wasn't sure if he would have considered it, seeing as how he had left things with my mom before I was born, but he agreed anyway.

He had wanted me to return back to my apartment in Seoul, but I had vehemently disagreed. Despite the headache which didn't seem to be in any hurry to go anywhere, and a lot of bruises down my side, I didn't feel too bad, and we still only had a few weeks to finish the album.

I think the only reason he agreed was because we still had another ten days remaining at the retreat, and now that I had Inhye, I was able to rely on her to do a lot of the work. That and the fact the doctor had said I had to take it easy for a week—which meant staying in bed.

I'd agreed on that, only because I knew I would be able to work from my bed.

Or so I thought.

Even before I had been picked up and taken back to the retreat, one of the guys had confiscated my phone, iPad, and laptop, hiding it somewhere that I, bruised and still a little wobbly on my legs, was unable to go hunting for.

Lee Woojin had arranged for Inhye to also stay in the retreat with us, taking Minhyuk's bedroom and making him share with Dante. While H3RO spent the days in the studio, she was in the house, continuing to work, but making sure to keep an eye on me.

I wasn't too bad for the first week: I spent most of it asleep.

By the eighth day, I was going crazy.

By the last day at the retreat, I had decided enough was enough. After a shower which made me feel a little more human, I put on a dress and some makeup. Dressing was a little harder than I wanted to admit. I was still bruised along one side, but it was more from being stuck in bed for ten days and not stretching or moving properly. After making sure my bags were packed, I made my way to the kitchen.

"What are you doing out of bed?" Minhyuk asked in alarm, up early as always, cooking breakfast.

"I'm done with that bedroom," I told him, firmly. "I am bored and lonely."

Guilt instantly washed over Minhyuk's face. "I'm sorry!" he cried. "We got caught up in the album. We should have visited more."

"You all visited enough: you were making an album. That's much more important," I said, shaking my head as I eased into one of the breakfast bar chairs. "I hope you've got everything done as we need to head back to Seoul today," I reminded him.

Minhyuk nodded. "We all went to bed last night," he told me. He glanced over at the hallway then back to me. After quickly checking the food, he hurried around behind my chair and wrapped his arms around me "Holly, we wanted to visit more, but Inhye is here."

"I understand," I promised him. "Much as I trust Inhye, I'm glad none of you did. Plus, you needed to be focusing on that album." While none of that was a lie, equally, I did wish I had been able to spend time with them. Even though we were still in the same house, I had missed them. I reached up, wrapping my arms over Minhyuk's and then twisted in my seat just enough to lean up and kiss him.

As his soft lips moved with mine, I couldn't stop a moan from escaping me. I had been missing human contact, but it was amazing how quickly he could make me forget that.

Upstairs, a door opened and closed. Before I could open my eyes, Minhyuk had pulled away and darted back to the other side of the breakfast bar. I shot him a questioning look. Since when were we creeping around?

Then I remembered Inhye, just before she joined us in the kitchen. "You're up?" she asked, surprised to see me.

I nodded, hoping my lips didn't look as swollen as they felt. "I am not staying in that bed another day," I told her, then shrugged. "I mean, we're heading back to Seoul today anyway."

Inhye tilted her head to examine me. "You do

have some color in your cheeks," she agreed. She walked over towards the couches before I could add further color to my face. When she returned, she was carrying my laptop bag. "H3RO are booked into the studio for the next three days to record their songs. They also now have their own dance studio; I didn't realize they didn't have one, but that's rectified now."

From the other side of the breakfast bar came a clatter. We both looked over at Minhyuk who had dropped a ladle on the side, but was staring at us with his mouth open. "We have a studio?" he repeated.

I looked to Inhye with a growl. "I hate Lee Sejin."

Inhye muttered her agreement under her breath then turned to Minhyuk. "Yes. I've had it given a lick of paint and updated the cameras in there."

Minhyuk's eyes went wide. "Excuse me," he muttered, before running off towards the bedrooms. As one of the main dancers, I was sure he was going to tell Nate, the other dancer, the good news.

"Thank you," I said to Inhye.

Inhye took the seat next to me. "Working under Sejin, I was aware that H3RO didn't always get treated the same as other groups, and I knew they were often left out of things, but I didn't realize it was this bad. I should have said something sooner."

I gave her a sympathetic smile. "That asshole it responsible, not you," I told her. "And we're fixing it now. Provided we get this comeback done."

"Next Friday, we have their makeovers scheduled with Jae, and the jacket cover shoot at the weekend. Then, they film the rest of the video," she continued.

It was going to be a busy couple of weeks, and

once the single released, it was going to be busier still. I didn't have the time to be staying in bed. "It must be time for Tae's cast to come off too," I suddenly realized.

Inhye nodded. "He's got an appointment this afternoon. Oh!" she exclaimed. "And your KPopKonneKt is at over five hundred percent, with another week left."

"I don't know what I would have done without you," I told Inhye, gratefully. "Thank you."

She gave me a small smile. "Thank you for looking after Tae."

I had forgotten that she knew H3RO's leader. "It was nothing," I shrugged.

"It wasn't nothing," she corrected me. "I know how hard you've worked, and it's just as hard as they have. You have their backs."

"Is it true?" Nate cried, Minhyuk beside him, both sharing the same excited expression.

I looked over at him. "Yes, okey dokey yo!" I replied before I could stop myself.

Both of H3RO's rappers stared at me. "No," Nate said, slowly. "I … just, no."

"I think you need to leave that one to Zico," Inhye muttered.

"Technically, it's Mino," I corrected her, and then scowled at them all. "And it wasn't that bad." When no one agreed with me, I rolled my eyes. "Yes, you have your own studio," I told Nate. "Inhye arranged that for you."

One by one, the others filed into the kitchen. As expected, Jun was the last one in, rubbing sleepily at his eyes. He was still wearing the shorts and T-shirt he had slept in, and his hair was a rumpled mess. A huge smile spread across his face when he saw me, and he started to bound over, but stopped when he saw Inhye behind me.

"I'm surprised to see you out of bed so early," I teased him.

"I'm looking forward to getting back to Seoul," he shrugged.

"I'm can't wait to get back, either." From the kitchen, where he was helping Minhyuk, Dante looked over at me and fixed me a smirk. "I've places to see and people to do," he added, in English.

"I don't think that's how that phrase goes," Inhye gently told him. "Places to go, and people to see." She turned her attention to the kitchen, gathering up some of the dishes Minhyuk had been serving up and taking them over to the table.

Dante sauntered over, leaning in close to me. "It was exactly what I meant," he informed me.

Suddenly, I couldn't wait to get back to Seoul, either.

# 제18 장

# *H3RO*

*Anti*

For the first three days of the following week, I only saw H3RO in the late evening. They came back to the apartment, exhausted and hungry, collapsing around the room, devouring whatever food I had gotten for them.

Despite this, they always returned in a good mood, or mostly in a good mood. I could tell that Tae was stressed, although he was doing his best to hide it from his group. On the third night, the stress had been replaced with a nervous energy. One which they all shared. As they had sent a text message when they had left Atlantis, I was already serving up bowls of tteokbokki. I looked up from the spicy rice cakes and frowned. "Are you OK?" I asked them.

They all looked to Tae expectantly. Slowly, he nodded. "It's finished." He set the laptop he had been carrying down on the worktop beside me.

A huge grin spread across my face as I set the cartons down. H3RO had forbidden me from listening to any of the album, despite the fact I had pointed out on several occasions that I *was* their manager. They'd still refused, and I hadn't pushed it. While I had been dying to hear it, I trusted them to deliver. Tae was too much of a perfectionist to let me listen to anything he wasn't happy with, even if he was nervous about it.

I bit my lip, the anticipation building as Tae seemed to take forever loading up the Cubase program he used to create the songs. Finally, he set a song playing. As the opening bars filled the room, I clutched at the side of the counter and closed my eyes.

The first song had a slow tempo, but a strong beat. Dante's strong, high voice filled my ears and I couldn't stop myself from smiling. As I did so, arms wrapped around my waist, pulling me back into a chest. I knew without opening my eyes that it was Dante. The song, 'Broken' was about a guy who had suddenly found himself alone. The lyrics were a little ambiguous, but I got the sense of irreparable loss: a strong contrast to the tone of the song.

The second song was the opposite: upbeat, high tempo, with an EDM track behind it. There was something so innocent about the lyrics, a first crush, that I knew who had taken the lead in writing them. I glanced over at Minhyuk, and found him watching me anxiously. I gave him the widest smile I could, and was rewarded with an excited seal clap in return.

The third song was a love song. A love song named after their fandom, 'Treasure', clearly written about them. It was beautiful. I sighed, relaxing more against Dante. I could already see a bonus music video for their Treasures—and I was going to make sure that happened, regardless of the outcome of their future. The lyrics were so touching, thanking their Treasures for their endless love and support, and how that was what kept them going.

I was struggling to pick out a title track myself, and hoped they had done that for me. The fourth song was as good as the others, only this one had me wanting to jump up and down. 'Let's Go' was the kind of song you'd play at the peak of a night and have the whole club bouncing. The speakers of the laptop, although good, did not give the song the sound it deserved. It was the song that would get everyone hyped up at a concert, where H3RO would get so carried away, that whatever water they had would be showered over the audience.

I had decided that was my favorite, and then I heard the final song. As soon as it started playing, I knew *this* was the one they had decided on. Like 'Who Is Your H3RO?', this one was another song of pure empowerment. Courage, strength and determination, but instead of coming from within like their previous single had declared, this was about the support that came from love.

It was called '상록수'—Sanglogsu, which literally translated to *Evergreen*. That was how they were describing this person's love. That it was there all year round, steadfast and true.

And then I heard my name.

The lyrics were about the plant, but at the same time, they weren't. Love, like the holly tree, would protect you from evil as strong as Poseidon.

The spikey knot which had disappeared from my stomach, reappeared with a vengeance. I should have been happy. I knew that was what they wanted, showing me how much I meant to them, and it did warm my heart.

But at the same time, all I could hear was how

they thought I was going to be able to protect them.

When I'd found out Lee Woojin's company was called Atlantis, I had been curious. Atlantis was a city that had once been great and powerful, until, according to the stories, the people had angered the gods and sunk the city below the sea, wiping it from the maps. H3RO saw themselves as Atlantis, and Lee Sejin was surely Poseidon, the angry Greek god of the sea. But a holly bush was no match for a tsunami, and I did not have the power to keep them safe. If I did, everything wouldn't be riding on this song.

I had to clear my throat before I could speak, but I nodded my head towards the computer. "This one," I said, my voice barely louder than a whisper, hoping that the feeling of dread that had settled over me wasn't translating on my face.

From the smiles that were being sent in my direction, I was certain no one had picked up on that.

"You really like them?" Minhyuk asked.

I nodded. "I can tell you've put everything into it. Your fans will too. We just need to finish up with the video and the album." I kept the smile on my face and tried to push the knot away. I hadn't lied: you really could tell how hard they had worked. The last thing I wanted to do was allow them to think that any indication of the limitations of my own abilities could be translated to them thinking they weren't going to succeed.

I turned in Dante's arms so I could face him and wrapped my arms around him. "It's amazing, Dante," I told him.

"I know," he agreed with a smug smile, before leaning down to kiss me.

He had barely released me before Nate had grabbed my hand, tugging me to him. He didn't give me a chance to tell him how good the album was before he was kissing me.

I think a part of me expected it to be weird as I kissed each of H3RO, especially in front of the others. But it wasn't. And, as far as I could tell, it wasn't weird for them either.

Well, apart from the sounds of disgust coming from Dante when I kissed Jun. Jun merely dropped me backwards, holding me in his arms, and continued to kiss me.

"Oh, get a room," Dante grumbled. As soon as Jun stopped kissing me and looked at him, Dante's eyes went wide.

"You're always telling me I don't listen to you enough," Jun told him, with a cheeky grin as he pulled me upright and started leading me towards the bedrooms.

"Now is not the time for you to decide to respect your hyung!" Dante cried.

I was too busy laughing at Dante's protests to stop Jun, but Tae stepped in; literally. With Jun pulling me along, I walked straight into Tae's chest and ended up letting go of Jun's hand. "Keep walking, Junnie," Tae instructed the youngest member, as though he had eyes in the back of his head.

His eyes, however, were fixed firmly on me, and his intense gaze sent a shiver down my spine. All of a sudden, he had me wishing *he* would take me away to a room. "You killed it with this album," I told him, softly.

"You like it?"

"I love it," I corrected him.

"I hope the rest of the world does too," he sighed.

I reached up, pulling Tae to me so I could kiss him. They would, provided I—and Atlantis—did our jobs properly.

Much as I could have stood there, kissing Tae, or any of them, for that matter, the knowledge that I still had some work to do to secure their future meant I needed to eat dinner and then return to work. "I'm proud of you," I told Tae. "Now come eat the tteokbokki before it gets cold. You've all more than earned it."

The adrenaline they seemed to be firing on wore off over their late dinner. Knowing their next challenge was to choreograph and nail a dance in a matter of days, they all retired to the rooms early. I was going to do the same, when my phone rang. It was Atlantis' lawyer, Byun Yongdae. "Holly, I think you need to come into Atlantis," he politely suggested.

"Is everything OK?" I asked in concern.

There was a long pause. "There's something you need to hear."

Yongdae refused to give me any more information over the phone. With nothing more than the ominous message to go on, I got changed and hurried to the office. My stomach was churning. Something was wrong. If the fact that Yongdae couldn't tell me everything was fine wasn't enough, it was late. A lawyer wouldn't be at work at this time if something wasn't wrong. I sent a silent prayer to the heavens that there wasn't any further fallout from the incident with Nate.

At some point in the afternoon, rain had come and set in. I packed up my laptop and made the short walk to the Atlantis Entertainment offices, bundled up underneath an umbrella.

Although it was late, the building was still open. With idols and actors, as well as staff, given access 24/7, Atlantis still had a quiet thrum to it. I nodded a greeting to security, then took the elevator to the floor which had the corporate lawyers' offices.

I was surprised to see Yongdae wasn't alone, and it wasn't a pleasant surprise. With him was my father. "What's wrong?" I asked, ditching all pleasantries and honorifics as I tried to keep the panic that was building from rising up and taking over me.

"I've been working with the prosecutor on Min Dani's case," Yongdae said, wasting no time in diving into the explanation. "We were interviewing her this afternoon in preparation for the trial, and she shared some information."

"What?" I asked, suspiciously.

Yongdae glanced at Lee Woojin who nodded a consent at him. Silently, Yongdae turned his monitor around and hit play. A video started playing. I'd never been in a prison, Korean or American, but I was sure that was where this was being recorded. On one side of the table was Dani, and on the other was Yongdae and a woman who had to be the prosecutor he was talking about.

"You're looking at prison time," the prosecutor was saying.

"I don't think I am," Dani shrugged with a smug smile.

"Kidnapping, assault, trespassing," Yongdae listed. "That's substantial prison time."

Dani sat back in her chair looking far too relaxed

for my liking. "It isn't kidnapping if you're acting under the instruction of someone."

Yongdae shook his head. "It is kidnapping, Min Dani, and it's serious."

"No," Dani said. "If you work for a company and you're following out their instruction to take another employee, then it's not kidnapping. Especially not when that person has a contract which states they are the asset to the company."

Yongdae and the prosecutor looked at each other, before looking back at Dani. In that moment, I knew that the next words out of her mouth were going to make my blood boil. "What do you mean?"

"I was employed by Lee Sejin to do what I did," she said smugly.

"Where is he?" I demanded, turning to Lee Woojin, my fists already clenched. I was going to find that man and throw him out of a window. The prison sentence would be worth it.

Lee Woojin let out a long sigh. "Sejin is currently in Shanghai."

"Then get him back here," I growled at him. "Or so help me, I will fly out there myself."

"That won't be happening," Woojin said, calmly. "Sejin was sent to Shanghai this morning to establish a location for a Chinese office. He will remain out there to build, recruit, and manage it."

I blinked at him, trying to process what he was saying. "You sent him away instead of having him arrested?" I asked in disgust.

"We did not call you here to discuss Sejin," Woojin told me as a dark expression settled on him.

I held my hand up, shaking my head in disbelief.

"I don't care!" I snapped at him. "That girl is the reason Nate was drugged, spent a night in the hospital, and then had to deal with the press. Jun would have been kidnapped and who the hell knows what could have happened to him if it wasn't for the *weather*. Kyun got caught up in it all too! That's *half* the members of H3RO! And it was all under Sejin's orders?!" I was shouting and I didn't give a damn how angry Woojin was getting, because I was livid. "I don't know if it's because he hates H3RO or me that much, but you're sending him off to China to let him get away with it?"

"Being sent there is not without consequence," Woojin finally exploded on me. "I have forbidden him from returning to South Korea and you are to replace him as Vice Chairman of Atlantis Entertainment."

"I don't want a promotion!" I cried in disgust. "I want him in prison!"

Woojin slammed his hand down on Yongdae's desk, the action making me jump. "Having Sejin arrested will cause Atlantis Entertainment's stocks to plummet and everyone working here, including H3RO, will suffer for it. Moreover, that is my son, and I will not have him spending the next decade of his life in a prison cell. This is not a topic up for discussion, Holly."

"Then what about her?" I ground out through gritted teeth. I was fighting back tears of anger and frustration: I didn't think it was possible to hate anyone as much as I hated that demon-spawn.

"We will be dropping the charges," Woojin replied, calmly.

"Are you kidding me?" I snapped.

"In exchange, we will be issuing a restraining order," Yongdae offered.

"That makes me feel so much safer," I muttered. I turned back to Woojin, not wanting to take my anger out on the lawyer. It wasn't his fault my family were this awful. "And what about all that you said about wanting to look after the people in Atlantis? Or was that all lies?"

"As I have said, I have done this to do just that, Holly," Woojin told me, his voice cold and unforgiving. "That is also why I am appointing you Vice Chairman."

"What about H3RO?" I demanded.

"What about H3RO??" he asked.

"This stupid deal to get them another number one?" I pointed out. "The least we can do is accept it is bullshit and do the right thing by them, at least here."

Lee Woojin shook his head. "The board are aware of the agreement. Sejin has only been reassigned to Shanghai. There is no reason for that to change."

I had to stop myself from responding to that. Instead, I turned on my heel and left the office. I went straight to my office, where I picked a vase up from the sideboard and hurled it on the floor.

Now I understood why people did that in the movies. There was something remarkably therapeutic about that.

# 제19 장
# *H3R으*

*Naughty Boy*

My phone beeped at me and I pulled it out of my pocket to read the email. Lee Woojin had wasted no time in issuing an internal email to a limited audience. Most of it referenced a local school. Effective as of Monday, Atlantis Entertainment would be partnering with Seoul Leadership Academy, a school where several members of Bright Boys were enrolled, including my younger half-brother.

Tagged onto the end of the email was a brief note to say Lee Sejin had moved to Shanghai to start moving Atlantis into an international standing. Four sentences including one wishing him luck.

The phone went back into my pocket before I could hurl it across the room.

I was so mad, but part of that anger was directed at the fact that actually, if it meant protecting the people at Atlantis, Woojin had done the right thing. I was just so mad that it meant Sejin would get away with it. And not just get away with it, but live in Shanghai. If he was starting up Atlantis Entertainment, China, then he wouldn't be doing it from a crappy little apartment.

I paced up and down the office, along the window, trying to calm myself down. I had so much fury coursing through me, I was sure it had replaced my blood. I also knew this was not the kind of mood I should return to the dorm in. I slowed ... how was I supposed to tell the others about this?

I rubbed at the back of my neck, about to resume my pacing, when there was a knock at the door. "Yes?" I called, expecting it to be security. On the few occasions I had worked late at the office, after midnight, they did hourly checks to make sure everyone was OK. That and the fact I had been throwing things around.

The door opened, but instead of security, it was Dante. "You're here," he said.

"So are you," I pointed out, confused. "Why aren't you in bed?"

"Why aren't you?" he returned as he stepped into my office, closing the door behind him.

I shrugged. "I'm working." From the light of the desk lamp, most of the room was still in darkness, including Dante. "But why are you here?" I asked, still confused. "Is everything OK?"

"No," he responded, solemnly.

Alarm washed over me and I pushed my chair out, hurrying over to him. I grabbed his hand, dragging him over to the desk and the light so I could see him better. "How did you find out?" I asked him, wincing.

Dante tilted his head and gave me an amused smile. "You're worrying about me." He then frowned. "Wait ... Find out about what?"

My shoulders slumped as I sighed. "The girl who tried to kidnap Jun won't be prosecuted," I told him. I didn't want to, but if that email announcement had gone out, it wouldn't be long before that information got back to H3RO and I preferred they got the story from me. "Lee Sejin was behind it. She's been released, and he's been sent to China."

Dante stared down at me, then, quickly, he stepped forward and wrapped his arms around me. He held me tightly as I clung onto him, grateful for his embrace. Even more so for him not asking any more questions. "Let's go home," he murmured.

I shook my head. "I can't. I'm too angry."

"Then let's change that," Dante told me. "Let's make you forget about it for a while." Before I could ask him what miracle he thought he could perform to achieve that, he leaned down and nipped at my ear. "I know just what to do."

Despite everything, my heart started pounding and heat started building. I slowly licked my lips. "That's an awful lot of anger to make me forget."

The look in Dante's eyes turned to what I can only describe as filth. He lowered his arms, making my breath hitch in my throat as his hands settled on my waist. Slowly, keeping his eyes locked on mine, he crouched down, his hands traveling down my thighs until they reached the bottom of my dress. Then the hands slid under, up to my underwear. His fingers gripped the bottom, tugging them down, slowly until they dropped to the floor.

I stepped out of them. Dante gave me a smirk, and then scooped them up, tucking them in his pocket. I arched an eyebrow. "Is that your kink?"

He stood, still smirking. "I have a few kinks, but that's not one of them."

"That's the second pair of my panties you've

pocketed," I pointed out.

Once again, Dante leaned forward to my ear. "The more of them I have, the less you have." In one quick movement, his hand went back under the skirt, cupping me. His thumb rested against me. "You're already ready for me, so why have that scrap of fabric in the way?"

Oh, I really was ready for him. When his thumb rubbed up over me, I gasped in pleasure. Dante's mouth was on mine before I could catch my breath, his tongue diving in. At the last moment, his other hand went around my back, holding me up—I needed it.

His tongue was rough and demanding, the opposite to the soft caresses of his thumb. My head went dizzy at the contrast, but his thumb wasn't enough. I ground up against him, trying to tell him what I needed without using my otherwise occupied mouth.

And then he not only let go of me, but he also pulled away. "Dante!" I moaned in frustration. Silently, he took my hand, pulling me towards the doorway. "What are you doing? Where are we going?"

He glanced back at me. "Find out."

I allowed him to lead me out of my office, partly because I was now curious as hell, and partly because I was now feeling exceptionally frustrated and I wasn't going to let this night end without an orgasm—not after that.

He led me to the elevator, standing behind me, waiting for me to push the button. I did, leaning forward, and as I stood upright after pressing the button, an arm wrapped around me, pulling me back to him. I could feel his erection in the small of my back, but before I could think about acting on it, the arm around me moved to my stomach, and then down, scrunching up the skirt of my dress, pulling it up. "Dante!" I exclaimed as his hand was once again cupping me. "There are cameras!" I protested, about to turn around.

"Only behind us," he murmured in my ear as his finger was teasing me again. I slumped back against him, mumbling something incoherent. The elevator pinged, and just like that, his hands were off me.

*Holy hell*, he was getting me so worked up, and then stopping, just as I was starting to feel good. "Are you kidding me?" I hissed in frustration as we stepped in the lift.

He rounded on me, backing me up against the wall. "I will push that emergency stop button right now and take you right here," he told me, his voice low and husky. My breath caught in my throat again, and I tried to swallow. I started to nod as his body went flush against mine, hard against soft. "But it's all going to be on camera," he added.

"I hate you right now," I informed him, closing my eyes.

Once again, he stepped away from me as the door pinged open. He stepped out into the corridor, and my body took on a life of its own, following behind. I would have liked the ability to leave him there and head back to the dorm, but damn it, that was not going to happen.

Dante led me down the corridors to the deserted canteen, and I paused in the doorway with a frown. "Food?" I asked, my voice echoing around the dark, empty room. "Is that your kink?" I added, dropping my words to a whisper.

"Nope," he said, smirking again, as he took my

hand, leading me through the tables. It wasn't until he reached the tall ones at the back that he stopped. He leaned towards me. "You might want to keep your voice down," he whispered in my ear.

"What do you mean by that?" I demanded.

Dante claimed my mouth with his instead of answering me. I pressed my hand against his chest and pushed myself away. "The cameras—"

"Blind spot," he murmured before kissing me again.

Atlantis had cameras everywhere. The only places they didn't seem to be, aside from the bathrooms, were in mine, Sejin's and Woojin's offices. I pressed my hand against him once more so I could step back and look around. I could see the cameras, but, as Dante had said, they didn't seem to be pointing just here. I stepped to the side, spotting one behind an enormous oversized bush, then frowned. "Did you move that plant?" I asked, sure that the last time I had been here it had been to one side.

Dante nodded. "Right here, no one can see us." He reached down, put his hands around my waist, and then picked me up. He turned, setting me on top of the tall table, and stared up at me with a suspiciously evil looking grin. "But they sure as hell can hear you."

My eyes went wide, as I turned to look down below. The table, right on the edge of the room, overlooked the main entrance. I'd sat two tables over with Lee Woojin and seen the view below. As it was, the still functioning entrance was all lit up—the light was what was illuminating the canteen, albeit dimly. And directly below us, now manned by three security guards instead of the two receptionists, was the welcome desk.

As I paused, holding my breath, I realized I could hear the low murmur of their conversation.

I opened my mouth to protest, just as Dante tugged me to the end of the table and spread my legs. It took everything in me not to squeal at the motion. "Dante!" I hissed.

"Sound travels in here," he informed me with that wicked smirked. Then his mouth went straight between my legs. His tongue ran along me, but it was his moan of pleasure which sent my heart racing. It was late at night and he hadn't shaved before coming out. The slight roughness of his stubble grazed along my inner thighs.

I had to clamp down on my lower lip with my teeth as his tongue continued to arouse me, sucking gently, then harder. My hands, which had been clamped to the edge of the table, gripped tighter. I was sure I was going to break a chunk of the plastic off. "Oh, hell," I hissed as his tongue did evil things to me. Evil, but so, *so* good.

"You taste so good," he moaned against me, the vibration of his voice rippling through me.

Desperate not to attract any attention up here, I fought hard to keep that orgasm away.

Dante fought harder.

Just when I was sure my teeth were going to draw blood, he slipped a finger in me, moving it expertly in time with his mouth. My hips bucked. My hands flew from the table to clamp down over my mouth, just in time as the explosion of pleasure hit me. My hands only just muffled my cries, as I was unable to stop them. I fell backwards, landing on the table with a soft thump.

And damn him, Dante's lips and tongue kept

working at me. He slipped a second finger in me. I'd barely come down from the first orgasm when he made the second hit me. This time, I sat bolt upright, my hands doing nothing to stop me cursing loudly—the only thing I could manage.

I slumped forward, my hands finding Dante's hair, twisting it around my fingers as I tried to pull him away. "You have to stop," I panted as his fingers continued to work in and out of my quivering body.

His mouth pulled away, and he stood upright so he could claim my other lips, but his fingers kept going. I could taste myself on him, and holy hell, there was something just as arousing at that.

Just as I could feel myself heading for a third time, his fingers slid out of me. I groaned into his mouth, partly from relief, partly from disappointment, then kissed him harder.

Once more, his hands went to my waist, picking me up from the table. Holding me gently, but firmly, he turned around, then settled me down on the edge of a table with a normal height. It wasn't until I heard the familiar sound of foil ripping that I pulled back. "You came prepared?"

He paused to arch an eyebrow at me. "Prepared was finding this beautiful location. This was a long-time overdue." He stepped forward, positioning himself at my entrance. I leaned forward, seizing his shoulders. With the light behind him, he almost looked like there was a halo glowing around him. The movement he made to push his way inside me was anything but angelic.

He felt so good filling me, it had to be sinful. "Oh hell," I moaned. "They're going to hear me."

"They've already heard you, baby," he informed me, matter of factly. Slowly, he started moving in and out.

I let out another moan, fully aware of it echoing around the room. "I hate you," I ground out as he quickened his pace. I had to bite down on my lip again as I clutched on to him. As his movements became harder, deeper, the table started moving backwards, a small screech accompanying each thrust. "Dante!" I managed to hiss.

The table hit a supporting column with a thud sending Dante deep inside me. The third orgasm hit me just as hard. "Oh god," I muttered, over and over again, as Dante continued his sinfully good movements, drawing out the overwhelming feeling. Finally, with his own cry, he joined me, muttering Chinese words in my ear as he jerked against me. His fingers dug into my hips, but I didn't care. The only reason I was still upright was because of him. How he was still standing was a complete mystery.

The action had my thoughts become more coherent, and the realization that neither of us had exactly been quiet and we were right above the reception. "I hate you," I grumbled as I started to get down from the table.

"No, you don't," he said.

I looked up at him, and slowly shook my head as I sighed. "No, I don't," I agreed. "I love you."

He grinned at me. "I know!"

# 제20 장

# H3RO

*Love It Live It*

Dante had indeed performed a miracle. I had been so tired, but also so worried that someone was going to make a comment as we had left Atlantis, that I hadn't even thought about Sejin. When I had returned to the dorm, I had collapsed into bed and fallen asleep straight away, so that when I had awoken, my head was clearer.

I was still angry, but I was no longer blinded by the rage I had been feeling. Instead, I was trying to channel the anger into something productive: making sure this comeback was as big a success as the previous; if not better! That being said, I had also decided that I was going to avoid Atlantis as much as possible. At least while those members of security were on shift. Instead, I continued to work at the dorm, enjoying the peace and quiet as the guys were busy at their new studio, creating and learning their dance.

By the time Friday arrived, the nerves in the air was palpable. This was it. The album was finished. All we had to do was a last-minute photoshoot and the second half of the video. After that, it was up to the world to decide H3RO's fate. I was that invested in these guys now, that I almost felt like I was one of the group, that this outcome would affect me as much as it would them.

We arrived at Jae's late in the evening, once again long after his salon had closed for the day. Yoo Eunjung was waiting for us with Jae, and she greeted me with a wide smile as I walked in. "Unnie!" she cried, bounding over. "Thank you!"

"I wasn't expecting to see you here," I told her, giving her a hug. When I had first met Eunjung, it had been here in this salon. She was helping Jae so she could get some experience, but her interest had been makeup. I had gotten talking to her during the previous comeback when she had admitted she wanted to be a makeup artist for an idol group. I'd told her that while I couldn't get her anything at Atlantis, I would happily give her a glowing reference. When the Chairman of Meropis Entertainment had called, I had done just that.

"I start the internship on Monday. I won't be able to help Jae for the music video shoot, but I wanted to be able to help him for this," she said, excitedly. She leaned over. "I'll be working with a new group who are debuting in the new year," she whispered.

"I'm so pleased and excited for you," I told her.

She gave me another hug and then bounded off to see where Jae needed her. I settled down into one of the couches to wait while Jae once again worked his magic.

Jae had visited us earlier in the day to discuss with the guys what they wanted. After Minhyuk had mentioned he wanted to try red hair at the last music video shoot, I had decided I was going to let them have a little bit of creative control for this one. I knew exactly what they wanted, and Jae had said it was possible, but now I was eagerly awaiting the end results.

For the first time, I hadn't brought my iPad with me, and I refused to pull my phone out. I curled up on the couch, watching the members as they worked through various stages of makeover. It was probably because they weren't able to sing or dance, but for the first time in several weeks, I was watching them relax. Jae had brought out some beers for them, and they were all—even Kyun—having a drink.

Tae was done first. He was the one with the least drastic transformation. With naturally wavy hair, he had requested it be left as it was. No dye, no bleach, no straighteners. Admittedly, there was still a trim and a bit of styling to go into it to make it look natural, but the effort was minimal. I knew he didn't care for having his hair and makeup done, although he had accepted it was part of the job. This time around, simple was key for him.

He came and joined me on the couch. I started to lean into him, but caught myself at the last minute: Jae and Eunjung had no idea what my relationship was with the group, other than manager, and I had to keep it that way. He gave me a nod of understanding, then pulled out his iPod, sticking his earbuds in. By the time the next member, Nate, was finished, he was fast asleep beside me.

"He has had the least amount of sleep out of all of us," Nate explained, giving his leader a sympathetic and grateful smile.

I looked up, giving him an appreciative look. He'd wanted to try something a little different, and I'd had trouble trying to envisage it, but apparently, Jae had not.

His hair was back to black, covering any trace of the golden brown it had been and somehow giving it a shine that had the salon lights reflecting off it. His fringe was straight and sleek, hanging to one side as it swept over his forehead. The side it had come from had been cut close to his head, completely opposite to the longer length on the other side. Through the short length, Jae had shaved in two zig-zagged lines just above his ear.

"That doesn't surprise me," I nodded, as Nate sat down on the other side of Tae.

He angled himself into the arm of the couch and then leaned over, gently pulling his leader against his chest into what had to be a more comfortable position. "Normally, this would have woken him," Nate murmured.

"He's worked hard," I pointed out. "You all have."

Dante was finished next. All the red that had once been in his hair had faded out. Jae had colored the whole thing a color which, in one light looked black, and in another looked blue. The style was kept as it was, hanging over his forehead with long, straight bangs which fell just into his hairline. From the wrong angle, you wouldn't be able to see his eyes at all.

Dante snatched the iPad from Jun, ignoring the outraged protests from the maknae who, under a head of bleach, was unable to take the device back, and started walking around the salon, taking pictures. "Dante," I said, in a low warning voice.

"Don't worry," Dante said, turning to me. "I'm only going to tease. You know I'm good at that," he added. From the angle I was to him, his eyes had disappeared like I suspected they would, and all I could see was his smirk.

I could have hit him.

Minhyuk got the bright red hair that he wanted, more crimson than the scarlet Dante had had. Unlike Dante's previous streaked style, the whole of Minhyuk's head was red. He'd had it trimmed too, but he still had much of the length that meant he would be able to tie it back in a ponytail.

Kyun was finished soon after. With his hair already half bleached from the last comeback, he had continued with the theme, only now, it was white. Not the pale blonde that came with extreme bleaching, but actual white. He looked like Jack Frost. Although we knew differently, it also looked like it reflected the cold personality people seemed to think he had. Next to Minhyuk, it was like looking at fire and ice.

By the time Jun was finished, Minhyuk and Kyun were both asleep, curled up on the other couch together. My mouth hung open in pleasant surprise. Jun looked so soft and fluffy. His hair was pink. A pale pink at the top, deepening as an ombre effect took hold. He walked over, snatching the iPad back from Dante.

Moments later, my phone bleeped at me and I picked it up, spotting the simultaneous Twitter and Instagram notifications. Sure enough, there was a picture—albeit in black and white—of the Minhyuk and Kyun with the caption of **[준] 엄마 아빠. #MomandDad**. The comments that had already received were hilarious.

I looked over to Jun who was grinning mischievously. He shrugged. "Kyunhyuk?" he suggested.

"Minkyun," Nate said, leaning over my shoulder to view the picture. I glanced at Nate who shrugged. "It's a thing, trust me."

"Really?" That was not the first ship that came to mind at all. I glanced back at the sleeping pair, then at Jun, who was taking selfies. Red and white did make pink …

"They've been working hard?" Jae asked, joining us.

I nodded. "Almost nonstop for months, but more so the last few weeks." I stood. "Thank you, Jae. They all look amazing."

"Especially me," Dante contributed from the other side of the room where he and Jun were posing for selfies.

Jae laughed. "You're nearly there," he told me. "You've got this."

## H3RO

The weekend flew by. Both days called for early morning roll calls. The album jackets were being shot, and this time, we were also using moving photos. I found myself wishing Kate was there, then, when H3RO stepped out in their outfits, with their hair and makeup done, the selfish part of me was glad it was just me ogling over them.

That thought quickly disappeared when I remembered that it wasn't just me, H3RO, and a photographer. Now that Lee Woojin had given us an actual budget, we were able to do the shoot with a small crew; hence the moving photographs.

Because we had a crew, this time, things were a

little easier for me. I wasn't running around after everyone, trying to help get things perfect. Instead, I was able to stand back and enjoy the scenery. *Holy hell,* H3RO were good looking and I found myself thinking for the umpteenth time that I was exceptionally lucky.

Minhyuk joined my side, tilting his head as he looked at me. "You look happy," he informed me.

I nodded in agreement. "Aside from the fact all of you come alive in front of a camera, and even though you are all being so serious for the shots, I can tell you're happy and enjoying yourself," I told him, watching as Tae, Kyun and Dante posed in front of the camera. I turned to Minhyuk. "Combine that happiness with the fact you're all as hot as hell, I'm one happy bunny right now."

A shy smile spread over Minhyuk's face. He moved closer to me, resting his side against mine. Slowly, two of his fingers wrapped around my little finger. "I'm happy too," he told me. He glanced down at his feet, before looking over at me, chewing at his lip. "When we're done with promotions, regardless of the outcome, can I take you out on a real date?" he asked. "Somewhere out of Seoul, where no one would recognize me and we wouldn't have to worry about anyone photographing us," he added hurriedly.

If we weren't surround by a crew, and already pushing our luck with our half hand holding, I would have kissed him. He was so sweet. Instead, I nodded. "I'd love that," I told him. "It would be nice to spend some time alone with my Minhyuk."

"I like that," Minhyuk mumbled, bowing his head again.

We stood there in silence for a while, watching

the others work, and then I got the strangest feeling at the back of my neck, like someone was watching us. I looked around, spotting Nate, who gave me a bright smile. I wasn't convinced he was what had me on edge, but I couldn't see anyone else watching us. It did, however, make me step away from Minhyuk, not wanting to push our luck.

For the rest of the day, unable to shake the uneasy feeling, I tried to keep a respectable distance from the members of H3RO, interacting with them only as much as a manager would.

I kept the same mentality the following day when we returned to finish shooting the music video. Seeing as we had the footage for the story part of the video, all that was left now was to add in the dance sequences. We had two days in two locations. One was a studio, the other was in the abandoned building we had used in the first video. Soomi wanted to go back there for continuity, and I loved that idea.

The day in the studio was a shorter day, but only because the location was closer. For H3RO, they worked just as hard, taking shot after shot of their dance sequences from so many different angles. Not once did any of them complain, even when I could see how tired they were getting.

We also still had the minibus drivers who doubled up as security. The first day was on location, and a long drive. We barely had any time in the dorms from the photoshoot before we had to be up early, *really* early, to get to the location. I took advantage of the driver and slept most of the way there. The journey back was spent putting the finishing touches to my plan for Bright Boys. When Lee Woojin replied with a positive response telling me that I could take charge of the group and work with their manager, I set up meetings with the members for the following day, arranging for Inhye to go to the final music video shot with H3RO instead of me.

# 제21 장

# H3R오

*She's Back*

O n the second day of the video shoot, I decided to stay behind in Seoul. Much as I wanted to watch their dancing, I had other matters to attend to. Namely, Bright Boys. I had promised my younger half-brother I would look into the group, and so far, I hadn't. Now, with Sejin gone, and Atlantis partnering up with a school, I had an idea of how to help them.

If felt strange to spend the day with a different group. Bright Boys were a seven-member group. While some of the members were still young enough to be in school, Koreans stayed in school until they were nineteen or twenty, depending on when their birthdays fell.

Even though it was late when I finally left the office, I'd received a message from Inhye to say that they had left the location and were on their way home. I would still beat them back. Knowing they would be tired and hungry, I picked up some food and a lot of soju, and made my way back to the apartment.

I was exhausted, and already questioning my sanity at taking on the Bright Boys problem. Their leader, Hyunseo, had been arrested for assault, and the lawyers had said unless he gave a reason as to why he attacked someone, he was going to end up in prison. I'd met with him and tried everything I could to get him to open up, but he had remained like a locked box.

I made the hardest decision then. I disbanded Bright Boys and told the younger members who had barely attended school over the last couple of years, to return to the Seoul Leadership Academy Lee Woojin had partnered with. Needless to say, that hadn't been a pleasant experience, and even though I had asked the members to trust me, none of them did. Lee Seungjin, the younger half-brother who I was genuinely trying to help, cussed me out and decided he wanted nothing more to do with me.

Hence the soju.

I stepped out of the elevator, my arms weighed down with bottles and takeaway containers, and set them down on the floor so that I could key in the code to unlock the door to the dorm. I sighed when I realized it was already unlocked. The team must have made good time getting home.

At the thought of seeing the guys sooner than I thought, my mood perked up. I was still in awe at the fact being in a relationship with all six of them was a possibility … no, a reality …

*Somehow,* this was working.

I loved them all, and I loved them all equally. Just as importantly, I knew that they loved me, and they loved each other. It was completely different, but the seven of us got different types of intimacy from each other. Just because they weren't sleeping with each other, didn't mean they didn't love each other.

It wasn't easy, and there were definitely times when I could see some of the guys, Kyun and Minhyuk in particular, struggling when they saw me with the others. However, aside from the usual bickering within the group, and the inevitable arguments of six guys living and working together on schedules which didn't allow for much free time, things were … good.

My heart continued to swell at the thought of returning home to them. I scooped the takeaway and alcohol up and stepped into the dorm. The dorm was hidden in darkness.

I frowned, using the light from the outer hallway to see where I was setting the items down on the kitchen work counter, then hurried over to switch the light on. As the light illuminated the kitchen, I pulled my phone out, checking the time. It was nearly ten. They'd had to leave for the location at two in the morning, after only a few hours' sleep. I shouldn't have been surprised that they'd all come in and crashed.

"It's a good job we've got a double-coded main entrance," I muttered to the empty room. The takeout I'd brought back was sushi. While it wouldn't be quite as fresh the following day, it would keep in the fridge overnight. I ate a few pieces, then put the rest into the fridge, along with most of the soju.

If the others were asleep, a distraction wasn't coming. I was going to pull on a pair of sweatpants and a hoodie and head up to the roof to drink in the cold, yet fresh air. I left the bottles on the side, then hurried along to my room. I flicked on the light, and froze in a confused horror.

My room was trashed.

All the drawers and the closet were open, and

things strewn everywhere. My mouth fell open as I stared, trying to understand what I was seeing. This was an idol dorm. The only people who had access were the other idol groups living in the building—none of which shared this floor—and a few Atlantis employees. H3RO didn't even have a cleaner, and in the whole time I'd been here, I'd only ever seen a couple of members of Onyx drop by. Even Seungjin hadn't been here while I had. And I didn't, for one moment, think any of them had done anything like this.

Was it a prank and they'd gotten the wrong room?

No sooner had that thought crossed my mind, it disappeared. Written on the wall, in what looked like red paint, was something in Hangul, which took me a moment to translate: *whore.*

My blood ran cold.

I backed out of the room, trying to keep calm. My first thought wasn't for myself: it was the others. I backed out of the room and darted into the room next to mine: the one Minhyuk and Dante shared. Forgetting that they might likely be asleep, I pushed the door open, bursting in.

It was empty.

I flicked on the light and spun around, checking the walls. The room was empty. It also didn't look like somebody had been through the cupboards and drawers.

I was feeling marginally relieved when I opened the door to Tae and Kyun's bedroom. That feeling evaporated in an instant at the sight that greeted me when I turned the lights on. There was blood everywhere. It seemed to be centered on the two beds which had been pushed together many years ago. In the middle, lying in a pool of blood which was still glistening, was a dead piglet.

Above the bed, the hangul still wet from the blood it was written in, were the words **You will be slaughtered like the piggy you are!**

I screamed, unable to move, and unable to stop until a pair of arms wrapped around me, turning me from the gruesome sight. "It's OK," someone was telling me.

"Why is she screaming?" someone with a thick dialect asked from the door. There was a pause then a stream of expletives. "Get her out of there, hyung."

I was scooped up and carried into the living room before being deposited on a couch. It was only then that I realized the person who had carried me out was Xiao, a member of Onyx, who lived in the dorms above us. Behind him was Jiwon, another member, and he was already on his phone.

"Holly are you OK?" Xiao was asking me.

I had finally stopped screaming, but now, the shakes had set in as I stared in horror at him. Xiao gently started rubbing his hands up and down my arms, which was when H3RO bustled into the dorm.

"What the hell is going on in here?" Dante demanded, shooting a look of venom at the other Chinese person in the room.

Xiao sighed, standing, so he could face the group. "We came when we heard her screaming. I'm making sure she's OK," he explained as Jiwon stepped out of the dorm, pulling the door shut behind him.

"Why was Holly screaming?" Minhyuk asked, hurrying over to me. He sat down beside me, grabbing my hand, peering up at my face.

Feeling everyone's eyes on me, I sucked in a deep breath, forcing myself to remain calm. It was OK to be shocked by what I had seen but continuing like this wasn't going to help anyone. I took one more breath, then patted Minhyuk's hand. "Someone has broken in," I told them.

"Has anything been taken?" Tae asked, staring at me, curiously.

"I don't think so," I replied. "I haven't checked all the rooms yet."

"I'll go check mine," Kyun declared, starting towards the hallway.

"NO!" I shrieked at him, so loudly, it had him freeze in his tracks.

"Why?" Tae asked, carefully, not taking his eyes off me.

"It's a mess, hyung," Jiwon told him as he re-entered the dorm. "No one needs to see that. Trust me."

Tae shot me a look, and I shook my head. *Especially* not Kyun. Whether he could read my mind or not, he reached out for Kyun, pulling him back. "Let's all wait with Holly."

"The police are on the way," Jiwon added.

I took another deep breath, and then stood, pulling my phone out of my pocket. "You all need to stay in here while I phone Atlantis," I told them. The last thing I needed was for H3RO to overhear the conversation. "Do not go into your rooms."

I walked past the group, through the small kitchen, and out into the hallway where I called Inhye. "I'm sorry," I apologized, after explaining everything. "I know it's been a really long day for you already."

"It's OK," she told me. "I'll have some hotel

rooms booked for you within the hour."

"No," I stopped her. "We can't risk this getting into the papers a week before their single is released. I don't want the scandal. It could jeopardize everything."

"Holly, someone broke into your dorm. H3RO aren't in the wrong here."

I chewed at my lip before finally admitting to her the one bit of detail I had been hiding. "They went into my room and wrote 'whore' on the wall."

"You're their manager," Inhye exclaimed. "That's ridiculous."

"I just …" I sighed. "I don't want a scandal. I'm not even sure we can stop this story breaking, but we need to try."

"I will talk to the team and see if we can come up with a solution. I'll also organize for a new bed to be delivered tomorrow and for the room to be cleaned professionally."

I leaned back against the wall, sighing as I hung up the phone. Honestly, I wanted to break down and cry. I didn't regret a single second I had spent with H3RO, but I was exhausted. All I seemed to do was fight all day long to show the world just how incredible these guys were and I was tired. H3RO were too. And now, on top of it all, they had to contend with this level of bullshit.

Someone had broken into their home. This was a secure building with all kinds of levels of security, and *still* someone had gotten in. My room had been trashed, but it was nothing compared to what was in Tae and Kyun's room. Their little slice of sanctuary had been violated. How could Kyun, who had trouble sleeping anyway, feel comfortable in there now? Yet, at the same time, if we left the dorms now, it would be all over the news.

Beside me the door opened and I looked up to find Tae stepping out. He closed the door behind him, then moved in front of me, resting his hands on my shoulders. "How bad is it?"

"Bad," I admitted. "Someone left a dead piglet in the middle of your bed and essentially threatened to kill Kyun." Tae swore loudly. He turned, took a few paces away from me, then swung at the wall. "Tae!" I exclaimed, darting over, grabbing his fist. "Don't hurt yourself."

"I want to find the person who did this and—"

"I know," I told him. "But you can't. We're going to have to let the police handle this."

"What are we going to do in the meantime?" he demanded. "We can't stay here."

I stared up at him, his intense dark eyes unblinking, and then I sighed. To hell with the scandal. To hell with the number one. H3RO's safety and wellbeing was more important than that. "We're going to deal with the police, and then we're checking into a hotel." Before I could change my mind, I pulled my phone back out of my pocket. "Change of plans," I told Inhye. "I need a hotel suite. I don't care how many bedrooms; we'll double up if needed, but I want us all to be together."

"Consider it done," Inhye told me. "I'll have the drivers with you soon. I also have the head of security coming out to meet you and the police now."

I hung up and returned the phone to my pocket, just as Tae wrapped his arms around me. "Are you OK?" he asked me.

I shrugged into him. "Not really."

The door opened once more and this time, Dante stepped out. He looked at us both and sighed. "That bad?" I nodded. "Xiao said we should go up to their dorms and wait there. I think it might be a good idea to keep us out of the way while the police are here."

"I agree," I told him. Knowing the guys as well as I did, I doubted any of them would be able to sleep, but it would give them the opportunity if they needed it. "But I would rather you all go to a hotel together and stay there, out of the way. That way if any of you do manage to get some sleep, I won't have to wake any of you, or disturb the rest of Onyx. There will be a driver downstairs for you soon."

Dante nodded. "I'll let the others know."

After he disappeared back inside the dorm, I looked up to Tae, finding him frowning at me. "I'm staying," he declared, firmly.

I sighed, but didn't object. I had been expecting that anyway. "I think Kyun might need to stay too. He needs to know what happened. We can't hide something like this from him."

Wearily, I followed after Dante, Tae close behind me. While I hadn't expected protests at being removed from the dorm, I had expected some noise when we walked back in. What I got was silence. It took me a second to realize that everyone in the room was staring at something that wasn't me.

That something was a woman.

And she had Kyun's back pressed up against her chest, holding him in place with a knife to the throat.

# 제22 장

# H3RO

*Justice*

Thinking as quickly as I could, I shoved Tae backwards, back out into the corridor, but not shutting the door completely on him. The commotion finally had everyone looking at me, including the knife wielding maniac. "And here's the whore!" she snarled.

"I sometimes go by Holly, too," I told her, cursing myself for not thinking to check there was someone still in the apartment.

"You're the one fucking all of H3RO," she declared.

"I'm H3RO's manager," I pointed out.

She glowered at me, the knife digging into Kyun enough to draw blood. I finally looked at her hostage, catching Kyun wince, though his terrified gaze was fixed on me as he tried not to move and make it worse. "I've seen you with them all."

"She's our manager!" Jun snapped at her. "Of course, she's with all of us."

"You can't pretend that none of you don't know about it," she snarled. "I know she's had you in her office. Just like she had him," the moment she pointed at Dante, I could feel the blood rush from my head.

"What's it got to do with you?" Nate asked her before I could say anything. I looked at him, mortified. He was as good as confessing it was true; in front of Xiao and Jiwon too!

I could feel the gazes of the two members of Onyx flick to me, but Nate's words triggered something in me. "Why are you here?" I asked her. "If you were that bothered about me being with any of these guys, you would have that knife at my neck."

"My deal wasn't to hurt you. The pictures will do that. I just want to do the world a favor and kill this little piggy," she shrugged, the motion once again digging the knife deeper into Kyun's neck. A thick bead of blood started pooling at the blade before trickling down his neck.

"What deal?" I demanded.

She looked around at all of us, then shrugged, once again letting more blood free. "H3RO is a drain on Atlantis. If I could find a way to prove that to the world, I was promised this one." She grinned, the expression making her look almost possessed. "It didn't take much following you around to work out you're a cheap whore, fucking them all. Only I've got the pictures to prove it."

In that moment, I knew exactly who was behind all this: Sejin. I didn't care if the Yellow Sea and an inability to speak Chinese was between us, I was going to Shanghai and I was going to put a knife to *his* damn throat. I opened my mouth, ready to ask her to let Kyun go, but I stared at her face instead. "I recognize you!" I exclaimed. "You're employed by Atlantis?" She had been on the sets all week. "Sohyeon?"

She looked surprised that I knew that, though she didn't confirm my suspicion. Which meant she had access to a lot of information. "That's not important."

"Look," I said, holding my hands up as blue flashing lights started illuminating up the buildings outside. "You have a room full of witnesses, and if you've been in here all along, you also know that's the police outside. I'm not a lawyer, but I do know letting Kyun go will work out much better for you."

On cue, the elevator pinged open and I could hear movement and hushed voices in the corridor as Tae quickly filled the police in on what was happening inside. Out of the corner of my eye, I caught Dante signaling something to Nate. I wanted to yell at them not to do anything, that it would endanger Kyun as well as themselves, but I also didn't want to draw attention to them.

Then several things seemed to happen at once.

From the hallway, someone called "Police!"

At the same time, Kyun went dead in Sohyeon's arms. I yelled his name in horror, watching him fall to the floor, the knife scraping up by his ear and letting out a thin line of blood.

Sohyeon stared in shock, her eyes wide, frozen on the spot.

Nate and Dante launched themselves at her. Nate grabbed her arm, twisting it back so she cried out in pain dropping the knife. At the same time, Dante body slammed her into the wall behind them, so hard, I thought they were going to go through it.

## H3RO

Hours later, we checked into a hotel on the far side of Gangnam. We were all exhausted and barely able to stay awake. Aside from Kyun who had been whisked away to the hospital, and Dante who had gone with him, the rest of us had to wait for the police to take our statements. Inhye had gone to the hospital to meet and wait with Kyun and Dante while I repeated myself many times over. It was almost lunchtime before we were free to go.

I sat in the back of the minibus between Tae and Jun, barely conscious, but so far past tired that I couldn't sleep. We had driven via the hospital to pick up Kyun and Dante. Aside from a cut to the neck which, thankfully, didn't need stitches, he was OK. He had faked fainting to help Dante and Nate out. Kyun had insisted he was not spending a night in the hospital and as such, had been discharged.

We checked into a hotel under a blanket of paparazzi. They had been waiting for us to leave the dorms, presumably witnessing Sohyeon being escorted out by the police, and they had also been waiting at the hospital. So much for avoiding any form of scandal.

The suite we had been given was luxurious, but only had three bedrooms. Glancing around the room, I don't think anyone cared. When I glanced into one of the bedrooms and saw the enormous beds would easily sleep four of them, I didn't think it would be a problem.

Inhye had somehow managed to arrange for a change of clothes to be left for us and I hurried through a hot shower, trying to scrub the traces of what felt like Sohyeon lingering on my skin, even though she had never touched me.

All through the police questions, I had kept myself awake fueled by rage. I had every intention of finding Lee Woojin and making sure he pressed charges against Sejin this time. I wasn't going to stand for anything less.

Only, when I stepped out of the shower and looked at the fresh clothes versus the nightgown, I knew I wasn't physically ready to fight that battle. Instead, I did the next most satisfying thing and turned my phone off. I'd already had several missed calls from my father and I knew this would annoy him more.

I pulled on the nightgown and all but crawled into bed. Even though it was early afternoon, I had been awake for almost thirty hours. I had just settled down and closed my eyes when there was a knock at the door. I sat upright with a soft groan. "Hello?" I called.

Kyun's head appeared around the door. "Can we stay in here tonight?"

I nodded, expecting Tae to be the 'we' he was referring to. Instead, Minyuk and Jun followed him. I arched an eyebrow, but pulled back one of the corners of the duvet. Kyun dived in first, snuggling up against me. "Are you OK?" I asked him softly as Jun and Minhyuk got in on the other side.

"I don't understand why so many people hate me," he said, quietly.

I chewed at my lip, then sighed, reaching down to stroke his hair. "Kyun, there's something you should know," I told him. "Sohyeon is your anti-fan."

Kyun finally looked up at me, frowning. "But she was working at Atlantis."

I nodded. "I recognized the words she used, and when I mentioned it to one of the police officers, they asked her. She admitted she's been sending you stuff for years. Apparently Sejin did look into it, but only to know who she was. When she resurfaced after your last comeback he decided to use her to make sure you didn't succeed at this next one." I sighed, feeling my chin wobble as I fought back the tears. "And to get me out of Atlantis too. I'm sorry. If it wasn't for me making that stupid agreement with him, none of this would have happened."

"Without you, we wouldn't have had a comeback," Kyun said, simply. "I've never felt happier and more alive than I have the last six months with you."

"You've also been stranded on an island, received death threats from a psycho anti-fan, and also had her try to kill you," I pointed out.

"As you said, Kyun had that anti-fan before you," Jun chimed in. He was on the far side of Minhyuk, but shuffled up, pushing Minhyuk closer to me, so he could stretch his arms out around us.

"And we already had a career death sentence," Minhyuk added.

"But we didn't have you," Kyun said, softly. "And I wouldn't change that for anything."

There was another knock at the door, and this time, Tae stuck his head round. He had a frown on his face until he realized how many members of H3RO were in the bed with me. "Oh, you're all in here," he determined, cocking his head. "Room for one more?"

I blinked, then nodded. Tae strode across the room, getting in the bed behind Kyun. "You OK, little brother?" I heard him murmur.

"Don't forget us!" Dante exclaimed, suddenly

bounding into the room, Nate close behind him.

"I don't think the bed is big enough for all of us," Jun informed him.

Dante ran at the bed, taking a flying leap on it, landing on top of Jun who let out a loud 'oomph'. "Then you can get out of it, can't you, Jun."

Nate, a little more reserved, decided to lay across the bottom of the bed, using my lap as a place to lay his head. I glanced down watching them all get comfortable on the bed and around each other, and couldn't help but smile. This was as surreal as it was real. Despite everything, I felt happy, safe, and loved.

So, of course, I had to do something to spoil it.

I could tell Kyun and Nate had gone to sleep, and Minhyuk and Jun weren't far behind. I wanted to do the same. Unfortunately, there were two things constantly going around in my head whenever I closed my eyes: finding Sejin; and working out how much damage control needed to be done.

"You keep sighing," Tae announced in a low voice.

"Can you pass me the remote?" I asked him.

Tae leaned over to the bedside table behind him and plucked the remote off it, handing it over. I flicked on the television, quickly turning the volume down, then turned to a news channel. As I suspected, H3RO were all over it.

What surprised me the most was that they were reporting the story accurately: an anti-fan had broken into the dorm, attacked Kyun, who, despite being taken to hospital, was OK, and that she had ultimately been arrested.

Then came the news I was dreading. I had been

about to breathe a sigh of relief and turn the television off, but stopped when I saw my face flash on the screen. "…Suspect, Oh Sohyeon, claims that Holly Lee, H3RO's manager is in a relationship with all members of the group. We have reached out to H3RO's management company, Atlantis Entertainment, but have yet to receive a statement to confirm or deny these accusations. What SSKTV News can confirm is that Miss Lee and H3RO were seen entering this hotel behind me," the reporter announced, allowing the camera to pan around to the hotel we were staying in.

I raked my hand through my hair, swearing under my breath. Of all the things, a dating scandal was not something we could easily come back from. I had seen a lot of groups suffer when their 'fans' had found out members were dating. This … well, it was one thing to wish that they would be able to be happy for the idols they supposedly loved and supported, but to ask them to be happy for this situation? I wasn't even sure how well the international fans were going to take this.

"Holly," Tae muttered in a low voice as I tried to extract myself from Kyun and Minhyuk's grasp, while working free of Nate's weight. I needed to get to Atlantis to do more damage control than I expected.

"This will destroy H3RO if I don't get on top of it," I told him, finally wiggling free. "I need you to stay here and look after these guys," I added, before ducking into the bathroom where I had left the pile of clothes from before. I dressed quickly, hurriedly fixing my hair and makeup, then ran down to the elevator.

There was still a crowd of reporters outside of the building, but before I could step outside, a man was blocking my path. "Lee Woojin?" I asked in surprise as

I stared at my father. "What are you doing here?"

"My daughter had her home broken into for the second time. Do you really think I wouldn't check up on you?"

My hands settled on my hips as I glowered at him. "You let my half-brother flee to China instead of facing criminal charges, which, had that not happened, I probably wouldn't have been attacked for a second time," I pointed out, coldly. "So yes, I didn't think you would check up on me."

Lee Woojin's lips settled into a thin line as his hands slipped into his trouser pockets. "As I have explained to you already, having Sejin arrested will only hurt Atlantis and everyone who works there. Sejin will remain in Shanghai and will not be allowed to return home."

"How are you going to guarantee that? Confiscate his passport?" I scoffed. "And so what if he can't return home? He's still working for Atlantis. And what's to say he's not going to pull something like this to anyone in the China office?" I demanded.

"He is my son," Woojin snapped at me.

I stamped my foot. "And I'm your daughter!" I snapped back at him. "And yet nobody in this world knows that."

Lee Woojin let out an exasperated sigh, then grabbed my elbow. Ignoring my protests, he pulled me out of the lobby and into the first room off it. With the door closed behind us, he turned on me, letting me go. "I will admit that when I first had you come out here, I didn't want the world to know who you were in case you decided to go back to America, but now, I'm keeping that hidden to protect you."

"Protect me?" I repeated, dumbfounded. "How is that protecting me?"

"Right now, you are nothing more than H3RO's manager. Your identity is protected by their fame. The second I announce who you are, you lose that anonymity and the world will see you as my daughter. That's when people will follow you like they do H3RO."

I rolled my eyes. "You don't have to be famous to have a nut job following you," I informed him.

"I'm not worried about 'nut job's' following you," Woojin told me. "I'm more concerned that the world will find out exactly what your relationship is with H3RO." As the blood drained from my face, Woojin nodded. "So, it is true then?"

"I'm close to all the members," I said carefully. "That naturally happens when you spend all day and all night, working closely with them for months." I folded my arms.

Lee Woojin stared down at me, then he shrugged. "OK." Then, he walked past me, back out into the lobby. I hurried after him, biting my lip, as he walked out in front of the hotel into the arms of the press. "Hello, I am Atlantis Entertainment's Chairman Lee Woojin," he greeted the wave of cameras and microphones. "I would like to address a number of claims and accusations which have been made against my company, its idols, and its employees. I would first like to confirm that in the early hours of this morning, the Atlantis dorms were broken into and a threat was made against our group, H3RO, as well as two members of Onyx. Although H3RO's member, Ha Kyungu was injured during this attack, he has been discharged from the hospital and will be well enough to begin promotions for H3RO's comeback single later this week."

Behind my father, feeling so many cameras fixed on us, I was doing everything I could not to make any visual reactions to his words. I held my hands together, trying to hide the shaking, not from fear of being on camera, but from the unknown of what Woojin was going to say.

"I would also like to apologize to the public and to fans of H3RO, as we have, as has been suggested, been misleading everyone with the relationship of H3RO's manager, Miss Holly Lee …"

I thought I was going to pass out.

"… But not in the way that has been suggested. The relationship which we have been hiding has been between myself and Holly: I am her father. She has been acting as H3RO's manager to learn more about Atlantis Entertainment, but I am pleased to announce that at the end of the year, she will be joining me in running the Seoul based office as Vice Chairwoman, with her brother relocating to Shanghai where we will be launching a Chinese side of the business."

Lee Woojin wrapped things up after that, declined any questions, and then walked back into the hotel. Still in a daze, I followed him inside. "What was that?" I asked when we reached a place away from prying ears.

"You are my daughter," Woojin informed me. "But Sejin is also my son. I will not apologize for protecting him." And then he left me there.

I watched him go, trying to get my overly tired brain from running away with itself. Woojin had acknowledged that there was something between me and H3RO, then he had gone out of his way to protect it from the media. Was that my reward for staying quiet about Sejin? Was this the quiet before the storm: would H3RO suffer later? Was this just the best I could hope for?

Time would tell.

# EPILOGUE

# *H3RO*

*Idol*

H3RO were lined up anxiously on the stage for the final scoring on Mnet's M Countdown beside Monsta X and Momoland, both of whom had had amazing songs released at the same time. It was the first award show of the comeback and my stomach was eating itself with nerves.

Whether it was Lee Woojin's statement, or just dumb luck, support for H3RO had been appearing out of nowhere for the group. It seemed someone in a relationship with all members of a group was too hard to believe, and the public seemed to have rallied together to say that Kyun's anti-fan was making things up. When the music video for '상록수 (Evergreen)' was released, the number of YouTube views alone had broken all records for most views in twenty-four hours for any Atlantis idol or group.

The counts were good, but were they good enough when up against the likes of Monsta X and Momoland. I was praying that, because Monsta X had been number one the previous week, we stood half a chance this week.

The hosts were announcing the counts and I was

doing my best to keep up with my lacking math skills (seriously, not all Asians are good at math). I was certain I'd messed up somewhere when my total came to a perfect score.

"And this week's winners, with a perfect score of 10,000 are H3RO!" the host yelled in excitement.

My reaction mirrored H3RO. They were all stood, dumbfounded, on the stage, staring at each other as confetti and streamers rained down around them. It took Monsta X bouncing on them to make them realize they weren't hearing things. While they celebrated, I had to leave the room, darting in to the closest bathroom where I stood in a cubicle, bawling my eyes out.

They had done it.

That had been the first win. In the end, they achieved an all-kill, topping every chart. I was so proud of them. Their excitement lasted the whole of the promotions, and throughout it all, they stayed humble and thankful.

As time passed, heading towards the end of the year, I did my best to hide the growing sadness in me.

In between spending time at the various shows, I was in and out of Atlantis. I had finally collared Woojin and questioned him about H3RO's future, as well as my own. Theirs was simple: they would have their contracts renewed and I would be able to work with the lawyer, Byun Yongdae to make sure it was a favorable contract. It was even Lee Woojin who told Yongdae to remove the no-dating clause.

But there was a catch.

Of course, there was a catch.

And even though I was devastated to have to accept it, I knew it was the right thing to do: I had to give up being H3RO's manager.

"You're the Vice Chairwoman of Atlantis Entertainment," Woojin told me, much more gently than I ever expected. "You're not just responsible for H3RO now. You need to be able to manage your time with all of our idols and actors on our roster, and you can't do that when you're with H3RO twenty-four hours a day."

I had already discovered that when I was still trying to help the former members of Bright Boys, as well as Onyx who were about to embark on the first world tour for any Atlantis group.

It was also getting harder to remember that I needed to act indifferent around H3RO. It didn't help when the members could often catch themselves at the last minute.

I sat in my new office, staring at my desk, lost in my thoughts. I'd wanted to tell them tonight, but Lee Woojin had insisted on taking them out for barbeque. At the last minute, I had cancelled on them. I couldn't sit in that room with them and act happy, even if, in the long run, it would work out for us.

There was a knock at the door and Jun poked his head in. "You're crying," he stated. He was sat in front of me on my desk before I had raised my hands to my cheeks to discover he was right. "What's wrong, noona?"

I softly shook my head. "Nothing," I lied.

"Uh-huh …" He arched an eyebrow. "You cancelled on the meal and you're sitting alone in your office because nothing's wrong?"

I frowned. "Wait, it's meat … why are you not at the barbeque? Are you OK?" If Jun was missing out on meat, there had to be something wrong.

"You cancelled on the meal and you're sitting alone in your office," he repeated. "Crying," he added. He reached over, cupping my cheek with his hand so he could wipe the few stray tears away with his thumb. "What's wrong?"

"I'm sad, and I'm happy," I admitted with a shrug. "We made it. H3RO survived. Your contracts are renewed and there are already plans for your next comeback underway." Jun shifted his position, then pulled me into his lap, wrapping one arm around me, while the other settled on my thigh. "But in a week's time, with the new year, I start my new job as Vice Chairwoman of Atlantis, and that means I can't be your manager anymore."

"Thank god for that," Jun muttered, breathing a sigh of relief.

I leaned back to give him a questioning look. "Huh?"

"Those new contracts may have had the no-dating clause removed, but it's still questionable dating your manager."

The questioning look remained. "And dating the Vice Chairwoman is better?"

"Dating an idol is never going to be easy. Dating six of us is going to be mission impossible some days. But, as I said from the beginning, we can do it if we all believe we can do it. And something like this, I think it can only help us." He dipped his head, claiming my lips with his own. He worked his mouth against mine, then teased at my lips with his tongue. When I parted them, he pulled away. "I've barely seen you all day long, and all I want to do is be inside you," he whispered in my ear.

"That can easily be arranged," I responded with a throaty groan. My body was already responding to him, and all he had done was kiss me.

As though hearing my thoughts, his mouth returned to mine, and his hands traveled down my body to my butt, scooping it gently. He gave it a sharp squeeze, then lifted me so he could stand, before setting me back down on the desk. In the same motion, he had removed me of my underwear, tossing them to the side. A hand came to a rest either side of the desk as he leaned in towards me. "We're going to christen this office," he informed me.

He ducked his head again, though this time, he went straight for my breasts. The dress was halter neck and I wasn't wearing a bra: a fact he seemed not to care about as he wrapped his hands around my already straining nipples, sucking at one through the thin cotton fabric.

My hand shot out for the phone and I hit dial. It connected to Inhye who picked up instantly. "Inhye, I need you to not let anyone in my room for the next ten minutes." Jun bit down. "Holy hell," I gasped. "Hour. The next hour." I disconnected the call, just as Jun's hand slid between my leg. "You're an ass!" I exclaimed.

Jun glanced up at me, grinned wickedly, then started working his fingers against me. "I know," he agreed.

# The End …

… At least for H3RO's story

*If you've enjoyed what you've read so far, please, please leave a quick review on Amazon! They really help authors out and I (like H3Ro) would appreciate all the help we given.*

Sign up to Ji Soo's newsletter and keep tabs on the other groups at Atlantis Entertainment:

Bright Boys may have been disbanded, but Holly has plans for the members (February), and Onyx will be embarking on their First World Tour (March).

Head to
https://sendfox.com/JSLee
to sign up

# CHAPTER TITLES

The chapters in this book are all named after song titles:

1. *Baby I'm Sorry* by MYNAME
2. *Island* by Winner
3. *Jealousy* by Monsta X
4. *What Is Love?* by EXO
5. *Will You Be Alright? By Beast*
6. *Killing Me*, by iKON
7. *A Little Closer* by High4
8. *Make it Rain* by Block B BASTARZ
9. *Might Just Die* by History
10. *Bad Mama Jama* by Bigflo
11. *You In Me* by KARD
12. *Twins (Knock Out)* by Super Junior
13. *Lucifer* by SHINee
14. *Easy Love* by SF9
15. *Love Equation* by VIXX
16. *Watch Out* by HOTSHOT
17. *Oh My!* by Seventeen
18. *Anti* by Zico
19. *Naughty Boy* by Pentagon
20. *Love It Live It* by YDPP
21. *She's Back* by Infinite
22. *Justice* by C-Clown
23. Epilogue. *Idol* by BTS

# CHARACTER BIOGRAPHIES

# H3RO

**Name:** H3RO (헤로)
**Fandom:** Treasure
**Colors:** Purple
**Debut:** 2012-03-15

**H3RO** consists of 6 members:
Tae, Dante, Nate, Minhyuk, Kyun and Jun.

The group debuted on March 15th, 2012.

**Stage Name:** Tae (태)

**Birth Name:** Park Hyun-Tae (박현태)
**Position:** Leader, Vocalist
**Birthday:** March 1st
**Age:** 27
**Zodiac sign:** Pisces
**Height:** 182 cm

**Weight**: 62 kg
**Blood Type:** A

**Tae facts:**
He was born in: Incheon, South Korea
Family: Mother
If H3RO were a family, he would be the dad
Takes the role of leader very seriously
Protective of his group
Has a short temper
He shares a room with Kyun
Speaks Korean and Japanese

**Stage Name**: Dante (단테)

**Birth Name:** Guan Feng (关峰 / 풍관)
**Position:** Main vocals, visual
**Birthday:** June 24th
**Age:** 25
**Zodiac sign:** Cancer
**Height:** 183 cm
**Weight:** 72 kg
**Blood Type:** O

**Dante facts:**
He was born in: Hong Kong, Hong Kong
Family: father, mother
If H3RO were a family, he would be the rebellious son

The member who spends the most time in front of the
mirror
He shares a room with Minhyuk
His favorite food is chicken
Speaks Chinese, Korean, and English
Sleeps naked

**Stage Name:** Minhyuk (민혁)

**Birth Name:** Kwon Min-Hyuk (권민혁)
**Position:** Rapper (high), dancer
**Birthday:** May 24th
**Age:** 24
**Zodiac sign:** Gemini
**Height**: 176 cm
**Weight:** 60 kg
**Blood Type:**

**Minhyuk facts:**
He was born in: Ulsan, South Korea
Family: father, mother
If H3RO were a family, he would be the mom
Loves cleaning
He shares a room with Dante
The mood maker of the group
Speaks Korean and Japanese

**Stage Name:** Nate (네이트)
**Birth Name:** Nathan Choi
**Position:** Dancer, rapper (low)
**Birthday**: May 11th
**Age:** 24
**Zodiac sign:** Taurus
**Height:** 178 cm
**Weight:** 58 kg
**Blood Type:** AB

**Nate facts:**
He was born in: San Francisco, USA
Family: father, mother
He shares a room with Jun
The peacemaker of the group
His favorite food is sushi
Speaks English and Korean
Is no good at chat-up lines

**Stage Name:** Kyun (균)
**Birth Name:** Ha Kyun-Gu (하균구)
**Position:** Vocals

**Birthday:** February 3rd
**Age:** 23
**Zodiac sign:** Aquarius
**Height:** 181 cm
**Weight:** 65 kg
**Blood Type:** B

**Kyun facts:**
He was born in: Incheon, South Korea
Family: Doesn't speak about them
He shares a room with Tae
Often reacts to uncomfortable situations with anger
Does not eat meat, but will eat fish
His favorite food is ramen

**Stage Name:** Jun (준)

**Birth Name:** Song Jun-Ki (송준기)
**Position:** Maknae, vocals
**Birthday:** February 18th
**Age:** 23
**Zodiac sign:** Aquarius
**Height:** 175 cm
**Weight:** 65 kg
**Blood Type:** AB

**Jun facts:**
He was born in Hwaseong, South Korea
Family: Father, mother

He shares a room with Nate
Enjoys photography
Hardest member to wake up
Can fall asleep anywhere
Pizza
Previously known as JunK

# ACKNOWLEDGEMENTS

As you may have gathered from my dedication, there are a few idols I must pass my gratitude on to. First up must be Monsta X. I love these guys. Their music makes me happy, and I love watching them on the shows (except No. Mercy—that show broke me and I knew how it ended!). I always marvel at how fans can pick a "bias" (or for you non-K-Pop people, a favorite), because I simply can't choose. Which is what led me to writing this series: why should you choose if you don't want to? Now, H3RO aren't based on Monsta X, so don't stress yourselves with trying to match up the personalities. That being said, I.M was my visual inspiration for one of the characters.

Other visual inspiration came from Bang Yongguk (former leader of B.A.P), Song Kyungil (former leader of the former History). Kang Insoo from MYNAME, Kim Sehyoon (aka Wow) from A.C.E, and Son Dongwoon from Highlight (and Beast if you've been around long enough). Although I love all these members, I have not tried in any way to emulate their personalities—if that has happened, it is purely coincidental. If you're interested in discovering some more groups, I definitely recommend checking any (all) of these groups out. I've had all their songs on at some point while writing all my books!

Also, please, please, feel free to join me in my Facebook group and let me know who you pictured for each character. There's no wrong answer, and I LOVE hearing this back. I'll show you mine if you me yours!

Back to the people I actually know …

My publisher, Cheryl, who really needs to get out of my brain. As well as all the amazing publishing things, I've been listening to her epic YouTube playlist. She's also the one who has been building my website *and* formatting my books. The website looks great! It's full of so many goodies, including character bios. It's an ever-growing site, so the more groups you're introduced to, the more bios you will find!

Natasha, at Natasha Snow Designs is the talent behind my cover art. I simply adore all the covers in the series. Not only are the beautiful, but they also capture the story perfectly. Thank you for your amazing work, Natasha!! I'm already excited about the next books!

Thank you, of course, goes to Sarah and her continuous support from across the miles, ranging from inspirational pictures to pep talks at all hours of the day. And of course, all the "aaaah, what's that term / word?" when, after no sleep and a full day of work, I can't English ... (that's an intentional example of when I can't English). Or K-Pop (which is even more worrying sometimes) ...

A huge shout out goes to my life-saving beta readers and my amazing ARC team. I honestly love you guys. You've kept me sane and kept me going, and you are amazing!

Which leaves me with you. Yes, you reading this right now. Thank you for still reading this. Thank you for being part of H3RO's journey. I hope you consider yourself to be Treasures (a part of H3RO's fandom), even if you don't know much about K-Pop. Please do leave a review, even if it's only a few short words—they all count, trust me!

고맙습니다 (or, thank you!)

# ATLANTIS ENTERTAINMENT NEWSLETTER

Would you like to be kept up to date on the antics of the idols and artists at Atlantis Entertainment? Sign up to the Atlantis Entertainment Newsletter, managed by the silent Chairwoman of Atlantis Entertainment, Ji Soo.

Ji Soo will keep you updated on the Atlantis Roster, as well as providing you with a healthy dose of K-Pop, some Korean culture, and if she can persuade her 할머니 (that's Korean for 'grandmother', pronounced halmeoni) to part with some cherished recipes, some of those, along with some reading recommendations. There may even be a few insights into her crazy life. But probably not, because her life is very boring …

Find out more at:

https://sendfox.com/JSLee

# ABOUT THE AUTHOR

International Bestselling author, Ji Soo Lee spends most of her days lost in a K-Pop haze, which inspired her to start writing stories about her idols at Atlantis Entertainment.

Under the name Ji Soo Lee, you will find YA contemporary romances, with romance levels like a K-Drama.

Under J. S. Lee, Ji Soo writes steamier stories, mainly of Reverse Harems.

# WAYS TO CONNECT

**Facebook**
**Author Page:**
https://www.facebook.com/OfficialJiSooLee
**Atlantis Fan Group:**
https://www.facebook.com/groups/AtlantisEnts/

**Bookbub:**
https://www.bookbub.com/authors/j-s-lee

**Amazon:**
https://www.amazon.com/J.-S.-Lee/e/B07H353S3L

**Instagram:**
https://www.instagram.com/ji_soo_lee_author/

**Website:**
www.jisooleeauthor.com

Made in the USA
Las Vegas, NV
13 April 2021